It was fun.

Running around the train with Mary. I had a lot of fun then.

I don't remember why it was fun, but Mary and her mother were smiling.

That means I must have been smiling, too, I think.

They were good people, all of them. Mr. Isaac and Miss Miria, Mr. Jacuzzi and his friends, and Mrs. Natalie. Everyone in that dining car was really nice.

At the time, I didn't understand that, and I didn't even try to notice.

Now, though, I think I understand. But even if I don't, I'm at least trying.

It feels as if that train was filled with all th[e] things I'd forgotten.

That train may have been a turning poin[t] for me. If I hadn't boarded it—if I hadn't me[t] Mr. Isaac and Miss Miria—I don't even wan[t to] think about what would have happened.

Monster? You mean the Rail Tracer? ...Tha[t] red horror... Yes, I ran into it. Like Mr. Isaa[c]

MEMORY
THE BOY

at monster changed my destiny... But it
as scary, and remembering it is scary, too!
ven just recalling that creature is enough to
ake me feel as if my head's going to go all
range...

That thing was like absolute power and
rror incarnate combined. Something that
ould make any political or military power,
e will of God or the devil, and even things
ke fate and destiny surrender through sheer
rce. It was cloaked in that sort of fear—

·Did I just say something non-childlike?

You're imagining things. Yep, it was definitely
your imagination. See? Ah-ha-ha.

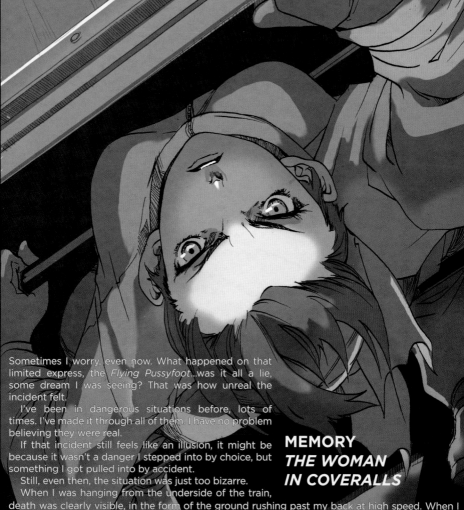

Sometimes I worry, even now. What happened on that limited express, the *Flying Pussyfoot*...was it all a lie, some dream I was seeing? That was how unreal the incident felt.

I've been in dangerous situations before, lots of times. I've made it through all of them. I have no problem believing they were real.

If that incident still feels like an illusion, it might be because it wasn't a danger I stepped into by choice, but something I got pulled into by accident.

Still, even then, the situation was just too bizarre.

When I was hanging from the underside of the train,

MEMORY
THE WOMAN
IN COVERALLS

death was clearly visible, in the form of the ground rushing past my back at high speed. When I ran into machine gun–toting mafiosi in Chicago, I had a clear sense of death there as well. Because I knew death's specific shape in those instances, I was able to avoid both death and the fear of it.

But the red monster *there*—that was another story entirely.

The circumstances surrounding that train were bizarre to begin with. It felt almost as if the train existed in a vacuum, isolated from the rest of the world.

And the monster seemed to be even more isolated, as if it were some sort of demon. One that stood outside the world, looking in.

The monster was pure terror. Its very existence was filled with death. It was a fear you couldn't escape, like being trapped in a nightmare.

However, in the end, the monster didn't kill me.

I still don't understand. Was it a good guy or a bad one? And in any case, was the monster really that train's...?

Train? What do you mean? ...Ah, the express with the ludicrously expensive tickets? To me, trains are only a means of transportation. Nothing more, nothing less.

Incident? Come to think of it, it was a bit noisy that night. However, to me, that's all it was. It didn't leave a particularly strong impression on me, and I don't have any thoughts about it to speak of.

I'm sorry. I'm entirely estranged from earthly life, and it doesn't especially interest me. That's why I dress this way. True, it does certainly make me stand out. For that very reason, neither people nor the world attempt to approach me. It's easier, though it's also lonely.

It was the same on that train. Only a few people were eccentric enough to speak to me...although one seems to have mistaken me for the Grim Reaper.

The train held a mix of people who wanted to die and people who wanted to live, although most people aren't either sort.

It is my duty to help people who want to live, no matter how bad they may be. As I said before, I'm estranged from life in this world. I may even have lost the concepts of good and evil entirely.

...A red monster? Unfortunately, I didn't see this monster of yours.

From what I hear, it saved the passengers and train from terrorists, so you could view it as a hero, could you not?

That the Rail Tracer may have been a sort of Grim Reaper... I would have liked to encounter it.

Since I was unable to meet that dark agent, I suppose it isn't yet my time to die. In which case, I'll simply continue to live—not that I want to.

Yeah, the conductors on that train died. Both of 'em. Huh? What kind of guy was the young one?

Well, let's see...

"What's fun about being a conductor?

"The part where I get to meet people. Some passengers I see only once, and others I see once a week. The *Flying Pussyfoot* gets a wide range of passengers, you know, from rich people to paupers.

"The differences don't stop at wealth, either; people with all sorts of pasts ride this

train. I try to do my job so that it'll be a train where all those people can smile. I just like watching people, plain and simple. Before I became a conductor, my old job was what it was, so now I'm happiest when I see people smiling and having fun."

...He was the sort of guy who could say stuff like that with zero shame.

When the train pulled out, he was...more enthusiastic than usual. Hmm? Why was that?

Ah. See, before departure, he'd spotted a real gorgeous girl by the freight car.

"If I had to describe her in a word, *pretty* would do the trick. She was wearing this black dress, and—how do I put it...?—she had a sort of mysterious atmosphere about her. I felt like, of all the people I've seen up till now, she had the darkest shadow. I thought maybe she'd never smiled, not once in her entire life. As a conductor, I decided I was going to make that girl smile during this trip, for sure. I think she'd be prettier if she smiled, personally... So today, I plan to work even harder than usual."

Yeah. He was the type of guy who said

that sort of thing.

In the end, though, that young conductor died. He got caught up in the incident on the train.

...Did the woman in the black dress ever smile? That's what I want to know.

Hmm? Me? My name's—let's see... The Rail Tracer. For now, call me that.

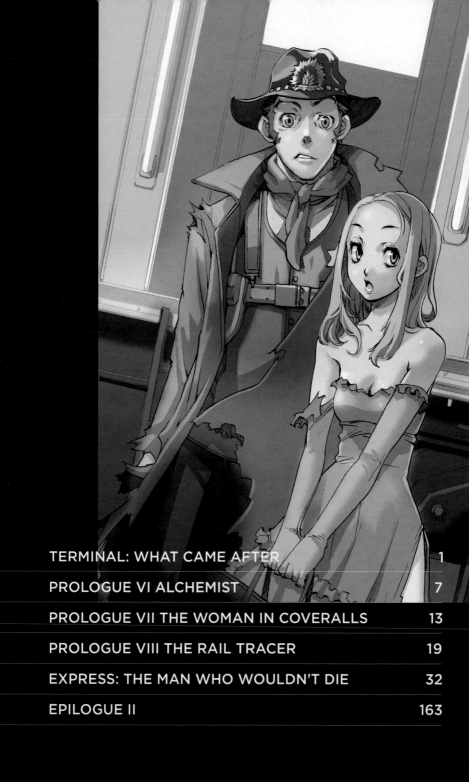

BACCANO!

1931 The Grand Punk Railroad: Express

VOLUME 3

RYOHGO NARITA
ILLUSTRATION BY KATSUMI ENAMI

YEN ON

NEW YORK

BACCANO!, Volume 3: 1931 THE GRAND PUNK RAILROAD: EXPRESS
RYOHGO NARITA

Translation by Taylor Engel
Cover art by Katsumi Enami

This book is a work of fiction. Names, characters, places, and incidents
are the product of the author's imagination or are used fictitiously. Any
resemblance to actual events, locales, or persons, living or dead, is coincidental.

BACCANO!, Volume 3
©RYOHGO NARITA 2003
All rights reserved.
Edited by ASCII MEDIA WORKS
First published in Japan in 2003 by KADOKAWA CORPORATION, Tokyo.
English translation rights arranged with KADOKAWA CORPORATION, Tokyo,
through Tuttle-Mori Agency, Inc., Tokyo.

English translation © 2016 by Yen Press, LLC

Yen On
1290 Avenue of the Americas
New York, NY 10104

Visit us at yenpress.com
facebook.com/yenpress
twitter.com/yenpress
yenpress.tumblr.com
instagram.com/yenpress

First Yen On Edition: December 2016

Yen On is an imprint of Yen Press, LLC.
The Yen On name and logo are trademarks of Yen Press, LLC.

The publisher is not responsible for websites (or their content) that are not owned by the publisher.

Library of Congress Cataloging-in-Publication Data

Names: Narita, Ryōgo, 1980- author. | Enami, Katsumi, illustrator. | Engel, Taylor, translator.
Title: Baccano!. Volume 3, 1931 the grand punk railroad: express / Ryohgo Narita ; illustration
    by Katsumi Enami ; translation by Taylor Engel.
Other titles: 1931 the grand punk railroad: express
Description: First Yen On edition. | New York, NY : Yen On, 2016. | Series: Baccano! ; 3
Identifiers: LCCN 2016035662 | ISBN 9780316270410 (hardback)
Subjects: | CYAC: Science fiction. | Railroad trains—Fiction. | Nineteen thirties—Fiction. |
    BISAC: FICTION / Science Fiction / Adventure.
Classification: LCC PZ7.1.N37 Bae 2016 | DDC [Fic]—dc23 LC record available at
    https://lccn.loc.gov/2016035662

ISBNs: 978-0-316-27041-0 (hardcover)
       978-0-316-27042-7 (ebook)

10 9 8 7 6 5 4 3 2 1

LSC-C

Printed in the United States of America

TERMINAL
WHAT CAME AFTER

1932   January   Somewhere in New York

"Welcome to our information brokerage. We sincerely appreciate your visit."

In a room lit by the dim glow of candlelight, a man dressed like a bank clerk spoke, smiling.

Although those words and that smile seemed ordinary at first glance, something about them felt terribly out of place.

The building was a small one, in an unobtrusive location in a corner of Manhattan. Officially, it was the office of a newspaper, and in fact, it did publish one. It was a small paper, with less than one one-thousandth the circulation of the *New York Times*, but even so, there was no need for the company to abandon its office.

The newspaper publishing business was conducted only for the sake of convenience: The revenue brought in by the organization's side business—selling information—was far greater.

Ordinarily, no information brokerage would have based itself in one location. In this business, the atmosphere you see in movies and novels—of people being slipped notes in back alleys and the corners of bars—felt much more appropriate. In the first place, once people knew where an information brokerage was, it could be wiped off the map at any time.

Even so, in addition to being a newspaper, this office displayed an information brokerage sign as well. It had a proper storefront, which, in a way, made it an embarrassment to its trade.

The fact that it didn't get wiped off the map meant there was reason enough not to do so, but the current visitor didn't pay the least bit of attention to that. They simply began to talk about the information they were looking for.

The man at the desk nodded slightly in response to the visitor's words, then showed them to a private room in the basement.

"All right. You've requested information regarding the 'incident' that occurred the other day... How much do you yourself know of what took place on that train?"

Speaking with what seemed like excessive politeness, the man from the reception desk began to discuss the visitor's request.

"It began in the dining car of the transcontinental limited express, the *Flying Pussyfoot*. While the train was in transit, bound for New York, three gangs of robbers found themselves on it together. One was a terrorist group dressed in black, commonly known as the Lemures. Their objective was to take the train's passengers hostage and demand the release of their leader, Huey Laforet."

Lightly raising his fingers into empty space, the man began to describe the situation glibly.

"Then there was a group of failed mafiosi in white. Their leader was Ladd Russo, a relative of Placido Russo—boss of the Russo Family, one of Chicago's many mafia organizations—and a skilled hitman. Their objective was a reckless massacre, conducted for money and pleasure."

The man from the reception desk kept talking, sounding quite entertained. It wasn't clear whether he was paying attention to his visitor or not.

"The final group was... Officially, they were simply called 'passengers,' but we hear that the presence of a gang of young people who'd planned a freight robbery has been confirmed as well. As an aside, they don't seem to have touched any of the regular cargo. In any event, these three groups came into conflict with one another...

and ultimately, victory went to the gang of young robbers. Are you with me so far?"

The answer to the receptionist's matter-of-fact tone was a quiet nod from the visitor.

"Well, well. That's very good indeed. It wouldn't be at all odd for someone who had been involved to be cognizant of the situation up to this point. In that case, if you'll permit me to ask, what sort of additional information might you want?"

Responding to the courteous man, the visitor slowly related what it was they were seeking. On hearing this, the man from the reception desk nodded, looking satisfied. It was as if these were the words he'd expected to hear all along.

"I see, I see, yes, I understand. What occurred behind the scenes of that incident: That is the information you seek, correct?"

Getting up from his chair, the receptionist walked slowly toward the visitor.

"It's true that, ordinarily, someone who was only marginally involved in that incident would want to forget it, but...if you were rather deeply entangled, I expect you wouldn't feel satisfied until you knew everything."

Even as the receptionist nodded cheerfully, there was a tinge of sadness in his eyes.

"Well, well. I do pity our president. I really do. The president is the one who most wants to relate the information you've requested, but wouldn't you know it, he's away just now. Ha-ha. These things never do go as one would like. I only thank God for the fact that I am able to tell you in his place."

The receptionist quirked a single eyebrow and smiled.

"All right. In that case, let me tell you exactly what it was that happened in the shadows of the incident that night."

Abruptly turning serious, the man got down to business with his client.

"Now, then: While you are here, you must not, under any circumstances, take notes on the information I am about to relate to you. It isn't permitted, so you mustn't do so. We will not let you get away with a single letter. We request that you keep this information in your memory, and nowhere else. Once I have told you everything, you may write down what you remember. At that point, you see, it will have mingled with your subjective view and will have ceased to be accurate information. Just think of it as a ritual that allows us to stay in business. Even if only in the eyes of the public, original information must remain the exclusive possession of information brokers and providers."

Having spoken that far without pausing, the man from the reception desk narrowed his eyes and looked straight into the eyes of his visitor.

"What I am about to say next is not simply a formality: I recommend that you refrain from investigating our information providers. —You will die."

Seeing his visitor gulp, then nod, the man smiled brightly and returned to his chair.

"The thugs aboard that train were truly suited to the epithet 'evildoers.' Of course, there were ordinary passengers on board as well, but the ratio was far to one side. However, the three groups of which I spoke earlier weren't the only threatening elements on the *Flying Pussyfoot*. Among them were individuals too far removed from the realm of human common sense to be called thugs. One was a contract killer nicknamed 'Vino,' a monster who has been conflated with a type of urban legend: Claire Stanfield. Another is—"

At this point, the man broke off, then spoke to his visitor as if testing them:

"Are you aware of the existence of beings known as immortals?"

With his lips still warped as if he was enjoying himself, the receptionist resumed his detailed explanation without waiting for an answer.

"Alchemists who strayed from their path and attained immortality... Technically, calling them *undying* isn't quite correct. To be accurate, there is one way for them to die, or in other words, one way to kill them. One simply has to put their right hand on another's head and think, firmly, 'I want to eat.' That's all. Just by performing that simple ritual,

one is able to steal all there is of the other immortal: their life, their body, their experiences, their knowledge, and sometimes even their emotions. They are able to take everything into themselves equally, through their right hand... In other words, to 'eat' it! —Well, whether you believe it or not is entirely up to you, but...it is the truth."

Having confirmed that the visitor wasn't arguing or scoffing, the man from the reception desk warped the corners of his mouth even further.

"And the name of the individual aboard that train was—"

PROLOGUE VI
ALCHEMIST

Ye gods. Life is going so well, it's almost frightening.

I've spent over two hundred years sneaking around and hiding, and just when the chance to "eat" them has finally come my way—I find myself simultaneously coming into possession of a large sum of money, one that will keep me living comfortably for quite some time. Incredible.

When I received Maiza's letter, at first I couldn't trust it. Szilard, "eaten"? I responded immediately, telling him I'd go to see him that winter. I'd had plans to visit New York in any case, so it worked out nicely.

The item I'd been researching… It was no more than a by-product, really, but it had been decided that I would sell those explosives to a certain organization in New York.

I'd initially considered negotiating with the military, but having my name made public would have been too much of a risk. This country's military is no longer loose enough to allow one to transact with them without revealing one's name. Since the "contract" renders me unable to use false names, as far as I was concerned, this was a lethal demerit.

With no help for it, I determined to sell the explosives to an organization in another country and had been conducting negotiations in secret.

Just then, I received two letters. Both were from old friends. Both had been sent from New York.

I panicked a bit, wondering how they'd known about me. According to the letters, both had learned my whereabouts from a New York information brokerage.

What a disaster. If even an information brokerage, in another city entirely, knew where I was, there was no telling when someone might attack and devour me.

I considered leaving that place immediately, but on reading the letters, I thought better of it.

One letter was from Maiza, a fellow alchemist. Apparently, he was acting as the accountant for some organization in New York, but he didn't write about it in detail. His letter said: *Szilard has met his demise, so rest easy and live without fear.*

Szilard. The name of the blasted old fool who promptly betrayed us and began eating our comrades when we gained immortality two centuries ago. Thanks to him, we scattered, and most of us live quietly now, for fear of being eaten by one another... Myself included, naturally.

I tell you, what he did was completely uncalled for.

If only Szilard hadn't been hasty back then—

—I would have eaten them all by now.

At the time, I hadn't given it the slightest thought. However, the painful days after we scattered and began to live separately greatly altered my thoughts.

I lived with a fellow alchemist who'd fled with me, but that life was a horrible one. Living in poverty wasn't what made it painful. After all, although immortals grow hungry, there's no need for us to worry about death by starvation.

The problem lay in the companion who lived with me.

At first, he was kind to me, but gradually, his hideous true nature began to reveal itself.

About the time we had begun to settle into a life of hiding from Szilard...he began to be unfairly violent toward me, regardless of how good or bad his own mood was. In anger, in smiles, and even in sadness: It sank its roots into our everyday life, as an act that was just as natural as breathing or eating.

As the days passed, these actions only escalated. No matter how badly it was injured, my body would regenerate, and he continued to torment me physically, toying with me, occasionally experimenting on me.

Even though becoming immortal doesn't deaden your sense of pain. Even though he had to have known that, too.

He gave various reasons to justify his actions. At the time, I was easily fooled by his words... Or perhaps I wasn't but simply figured that if I refused him, something even worse would happen. Back then, even if I'd tried to escape from that pain, I had neither the knowledge nor the courage to live on my own.

In the midst of those warped days, we received a piece of news.

It was a notice that a fellow alchemist with whom my companion had been secretly corresponding had been "eaten" by Szilard.

From that day on, his abuse of me grew worse. Initially, he'd tormented me with experimental tools, but from then on, beatings and other simple violence came to the fore. The cruelty of abuse conducted with tools grew until it was beyond comparison with what it had been before.

When I cast questioning glances at him, he grew more frightened than was necessary and strung together several times more excuses than he had in the past. I remember it felt as though he was trying to curry favor with me and that it was terribly ugly. When he registered my gaze, his face twisted even further, and he struck me.

One night, he tried to eat me.

It may have been luck that I was awake, or possibly I'd known that this was bound to happen soon. I shoved his right hand away with all my might, and a fierce struggle began.

Was it the result of my summoning up all the misgivings and hatred I'd accumulated? I was a moment faster, and my right hand caught his forehead. The next instant, my palm had absorbed everything he was. His body, his memories, and even his heart.

That was when my hell began. All I saw in his knowledge were his completely warped feelings for me and the terror that I might "eat" him someday. In other words, in the end, I'd been no more than an outlet for his twisted desires, and there hadn't been a shred of trust between us.

The things I least wanted to see, visions that made me physically sick, ate into my mind as my own memories. I found myself forced to live with that sinister knowledge, as if it was a part of me.

The notion of having been betrayed, while holding the memories of the person I'd betrayed myself—to this very day, I've lived in the agony of holding these two incompatible things at once.

In accordance with the principles of immortality, my mind alone continued to grow.

As it did, I was shown just how cowardly, filthy, and stunted all those who live in this world are.

At some point, I even felt a sort of adoration for Szilard, who lived true to his own desires, but I'm sure the blasted old fool would have considered me nothing more than prey.

That was fine. I, too, decided to think of everything in this world besides myself as prey. In any case, if there was no one in the world I could trust, all I had to do was use the whole of it in order to live. I even began to dream of giving everyone in the world the same sort of body I had, then devouring them all.

In order for that to happen, I would have to eat all the companions who'd been on the ship with me.

I'd assumed Szilard would probably get killed by one of his intended victims someday. However, no doubt I'd be able to pick up where he left off; in fact, I was confident that I could.

My shipmates had been kind to me, and it was likely that they thought I was still the same person I'd been before. On top of that, unlike with Szilard, by the time they realized my intentions, I would already be devouring them. My intent could never be communicated to any other alchemist.

The idea of having someone else attack me was terrifying, but when it came to my attacking them, I was confident.

I responded to Maiza's letter. All I wrote was that I wanted to see him.

I'd settled on the date and time for our meeting. Another letter finalized it.

The other letter was also from an old acquaintance of mine in New York. I'd thought he and Maiza had been in touch, but apparently, this was an entirely different matter. It was a letter requesting the explosives that were a by-product of my research.

This other alchemist seemed to be concealing himself in the Runorata Family, whatever that was.

It was a windfall. Not only would I obtain a large sum of money, I'd be able to eat him right along with Maiza. Not only that, but if I ate Maiza, I'd acquire all the knowledge Szilard had accumulated as well.

I imagined my wish coming true, and before I knew it, I was smiling.

I'd settled on a train to transport the explosives.

The *Flying Pussyfoot*. It was a unique train, operated by a corporation that was independent from the railway companies. A convenient train that smuggled liquor on the sly.

I scraped together what money I had at the house and succeeded in having a large quantity of explosives loaded onto the train.

The time had finally come to board. At the door, a conductor was checking the passenger list.

I tried to slip by him, but the sharp-eyed conductor stopped me.

"You're riding by yourself? Would you tell me your name, please?"

Having people pay attention to me for a variety of reasons is both an advantage and a disadvantage of my appearance. Consequently, I tried to behave in ways that maximized the advantages.

As a matter of fact, the man I bumped into a moment ago didn't make the slightest complaint. They were all so very *easy*.

Being unable to register a false name, however, is inconvenient. Making my expression and tone as childlike as possible, I politely gave my real name:

"—Czeslaw. My name is Czeslaw Meyer. Please call me Czes!"

THE WOMAN IN COVERALLS

That day, Rachel had put on her coveralls and gotten ready for a long-distance trip.

This time, the target was a special, privately managed train, the *Flying Pussyfoot*. It was traveling directly to New York's Penn Station, so once she was aboard, there would be no danger of a check along the way. After that, it would just be a question of how to stay hidden from the conductor.

In a word, she was a habitual ride-stealer. By now, she'd boarded more than a thousand trains without a ticket, and she'd gotten away with it every time.

She didn't feel a shred of guilt about this. After all, it was for work, and it was also revenge.

She worked as a gofer for an information broker, and she made her living by collecting information from all over America and selling it to him.

The president of the brokerage, who was located in New York City, paid his highest prices for "live information"—information that was communicated directly from the various cities. In addition, he preferred hearing tips in person rather than over the telephone. Apparently, this was because he could watch the other person's eyes, which made it easier to determine whether they were lying. He was an odd fellow, but she didn't dislike him. The offensively obsequious man at the reception desk was irritating, but she'd built friendships with everyone else. In the first place, it was weird that the brokerage was structured like an organization in spite of being an info dealer. It was probably only natural for its president to be a bit eccentric. That was what Rachel thought, and she'd continued to stay on good terms and do business with the company.

The president of the brokerage routinely asked Rachel all sorts of questions. He'd make her answer unrelated questions about a particular city one after another; he said he was analyzing information that couldn't be seen, as a rule. She didn't really get it, but as long as he paid for the news, she didn't care what he did.

Rachel was constantly shuttling between various cities. No ordinary information brokerage would have gone that far. In fact, it was rare for one to want information from other cities at all.

In the first place, under normal conditions, the train fare would be ridiculously expensive. If, on top of that, they didn't get any good information, not only would they not make a profit, they'd go out of business immediately.

However, at least with Rachel, this wasn't a concern: All the trains she used to get around, she rode for free.

"This is revenge."

That was what she'd once told the president of the information brokerage.

Rachel's father had worked as a maintenance technician for a certain railway company.

It was an extremely common story. One day, a damaged component had caused an accident, and the company had pushed all the blame for the error onto Rachel's father...even though the actual fault lay with the board of directors, who'd ignored the voices from the field that had requested new parts.

Her father, who had told them that not changing the component would be dangerous, had been blamed for the mistake. How utterly ridiculous. Even if he'd wanted to take them to court, he hadn't had proof, and his fellow technicians had kept their mouths shut, afraid of losing their jobs.

It was a laughably common story in any era. Rachel had grown up seeing her father burdened with that agony.

Loathing for one railway company had grown to include the railways themselves.

However, it was also true that her father had loved trains more than anyone. She vacillated between the idea of someday getting revenge on the railway and respecting her father's passion—and in the end, she'd chosen ride-stealing as her method of revenge. That way, she could damage the railway companies without harming the trains or the passengers. That said, she couldn't do any substantial damage, and it was nothing more than an act of simple self-satisfaction. In fact, if you considered the risk she ran in breaking the law, it wasn't self-satisfaction, it was sheer self-harm.

Even so, in order to keep her own anger in check, she kept right on stealing rides. She might even have been trying to find a reason for living in ride-stealing.

On hearing this, the president of the brokerage had smiled quietly and said, "That's a good thing. Well then, once you've found it, you can begin buying tickets. Buy enough tickets to cover the rides you've stolen so far as well. Just imagine you've paid the money to your father instead of the railway companies."

Buy tickets for her father. Would that day ever come for her? As she swayed back and forth on trains, the thought was always on her mind.

Today, all sorts of information had flown around Chicago. Stories of the trouble surrounding the Russo Family and the explosion at the factory outside town swept through the underbelly of society with the momentum of surging waves.

When she'd reported these stories by telephone, the information broker had said he absolutely wanted to meet with her and hear the stories in person.

The *Flying Pussyfoot* was scheduled to depart for New York that evening. It was a pleasure train built by some rich man. The type of train Rachel hated most.

It wasn't that she had no money. She simply refused to pay to ride. Today, in order to live out that warped conviction, she made for the station again.

She checked the cars of the *Flying Pussyfoot* carefully, particularly the areas around the freight room. When Rachel was stealing rides, these were the cars she used most.

However, at that point, she heard something unpleasant.

An orchestra from somewhere or other was going to put a guard in the freight car. As she thought of ways to cope with that, she checked the connecting platforms: In a pinch, she could climb up onto the roof or down under the cars from there. The undersides of the cars on this train were built to be slightly more spacious than those on an ordinary one. Thinking, *If it's like this, I should be able to get underneath with no problem*—something no normal person would think—Rachel gave a small sigh of relief.

Just then, she encountered a strange man and woman in black. They were dressed like orchestra members, but they had extremely sharp eyes, and no matter how you looked at them, they didn't seem like respectable people. For the moment, Rachel opted to make herself scarce, but she felt the woman's eyes boring into her back for a while afterward.

I think I'll steer clear of them.

As she thought this, she waited for the departure bell. Once she'd seen the conductor board, she crept up to the train, staying in the station employees' blind spot. Then, in a truly splendid motion, she leaped on board and crawled down under a connecting platform.

And then the departure bell rang out.

PROLOGUE VIII
THE RAIL TRACER

Late that night, in the conductors' room, the young conductor and the older conductor were idly shooting the breeze.

"Oh, you don't know that one? The story about the Rail Tracer, the 'one who follows the shadow of the rails'?"

Of all ghost stories, this one was a particular favorite of the young conductor's. This was because, although he was apparently no good at telling ghost stories, it managed to leave a terror with an unpleasant aftertaste, no matter who told it.

When he'd tried it on Jon the bartender the other day, Jon had just said "Hogwash" and left it at that. What sort of reaction would he get out of the older man?

"Well, it's a real simple story, you see? It's about this monster that chases trains under the cover of moonless nights."

"A monster?"

"Right. It merges with the darkness and takes lots of different shapes, and little by little, it closes in on the train. It might be a wolf, or mist, or a train exactly like the one you're on, or a big man with no eyes, or tens of thousands of eyeballs… Anyway, it looks like all sorts of things, and it chases after you on the rails."

"What happens if it catches up?"

"That's the thing: At first, nobody notices it's caught up. Gradually, though, everybody realizes that something strange is going on."

"Why?"

"People. They disappear. It starts at the back of the train, little by little, one by one... And finally, *everybody's* gone, and then it's like the train itself never existed."

When he'd heard that much, the old conductor asked a perfectly natural question:

"Then how does the story get passed on?"

The young conductor had been expecting this question, and he answered it without turning a hair:

"Well, obviously, it's because some trains have survived."

"How?"

"Wait for it. I'm coming to that. See, there's more to the story."

Looking as if he was having fun, he began to tell the crux of the story:

"If you tell this story on a train, it comes. The Rail Tracer heads straight for that train!"

The moment he said that, the other conductor's expression shifted into disgust.

Whoops. I might've sounded a little too cheerful there, he thought, but he couldn't stop now.

"But there's a way to keep it from coming. Just one!"

"Wait a second. It's time."

Saying this, the older conductor lit the lamps that sent a signal to the engine room.

And I was just getting to the good part, too...

Fidgeting because he wanted to hurry and get on with the story, the young conductor watched the other man work with sharp, intense eyes.

They spent enough money on this train. You'd think they could've set up a wireless between here and the engine room, the young conductor thought, but on seeing the lights that shone on either side of the car, he changed his mind. This train had been built with an emphasis on form and atmosphere, rather than function. To a bystander, even this practical signal probably served to illuminate the sculptured sides of the train. It was just the sort of gimmick you'd expect a nouveau riche company to come up with. And, since he was being employed by that nouveau riche company, there was no point in complaining. The young conductor smiled wryly, sighing over his position.

Just then, the older conductor finished his task, and, beaming, the young conductor began to tell the rest of his story.

"Uh, sorry. So, to be saved, you——"

"Oh, wait, hold on. Hearing the answer first would be boring, wouldn't it? I know a similar story; why don't I tell that one first?"

That sounded intriguing. The young conductor was nuts about stories like these, so he was raring to hear the other man's tale.

"So we'll trade ways to be saved at the end, right? Sure, that sounds like fun."

At those words, the older conductor looked at him, and his eyes were strange. Those eyes almost seemed to hold a mixture of scorn and pity. It did concern the younger conductor a bit, but hearing the new ghost story took priority.

"Well, it's a real common, simple story. It's a story about Lemures… Ghosts who were so terrified of death that they became ghosts while they were still alive."

"Wha—? …Uh-huh…"

"But the ghosts had a great leader. The leader tried to dye the things they feared with their own color, in order to bring them back to life. However, the United States of America was afraid of the dead coming back to life! And, would you believe it, the fools tried to shut the ghosts' leader up inside a grave!"

The content of the conversation didn't really make sense to the less-experienced railman, but anger had gradually begun to fill the face and tone of the speaker. The young conductor felt something race down his spine.

"Uh, um, mister?"

"And so. The remaining ghosts had an idea. They thought they'd take more than a hundred people hostage—including a senator's family—and demand the release of their leader. If the incident were made public, the country would never accept the terrorists' demands. For that reason, the negotiations would be carried out in utter secrecy by a detached force. They wouldn't be given time to make a calm decision. They'd only have until the train reached New York!"

"A senator… You don't mean Senator Beriam, do you? Wait, no, you can't— Do you mean *this* train? Hey, what's going on? Explain yourself!"

Realizing that the bad feeling he'd gotten had been right on the mark, the young conductor slowly backed away from the older man.

"Explain? But I am explaining, right now. To be honest, I never thought my cover of 'conductor' would prove useful at a time like this. In any case, when this train reaches New York, it will be transformed into a moving fortress for the Lemures! Afterward, using the hostages as a shield, we'll take our leave somewhere along the transcontinental railroad. The police can't possibly watch all the routes at once."

"Wh-who's the leader?"

Asking an awfully coolheaded question, the young conductor took another step backward. However, the train wasn't very big, and at that point, his back bumped into the wall.

"Our great Master Huey will be interviewed by the New York Department of Justice tomorrow. For that very reason, this train was chosen to become a sacrifice for our leader!"

On hearing this, the young conductor asked his senior colleague a question. He was still oddly calm.

He'd heard the word *Lemures* before. If he remembered right, the terrorist group whose leader had been arrested just the other day had called themselves the Lemures.

"…Why are you telling me this?" he asked the older man.

He'd thought he'd started to tell a simple scary story, but he'd stumbled into a terror that was far more real than any ghost tale.

The middle-aged conductor, Goose's subordinate, kept talking to the young conductor:

"Master Huey is merciful. I merely emulate him. Knowing the reason for your death as you die: You're very lucky."

Then, taking a gun from inside his coat, he wrapped up his story:

"Now then, regarding the all-important method of salvation… 'Everyone who heard this story died immediately. There wasn't a single way to be saved'!"

As his story ended, he took aim at the young conductor's nose and fired.

…But no bullet was fired.

"Wha…?"

A numbing pain ran through the middle-aged conductor's hand. The finger that should have squeezed the trigger pulled vainly at empty space. The gun bounded up into the air, then fell right into the young conductor's hand.

In the instant the older man had pulled the trigger, the young conductor had kicked the gun up, moving only his leg. Because the old conductor hadn't seen his upper body move at all, he had been entirely unable to predict the attack.

Having acquired the handgun, the young conductor shoved its muzzle into the forehead of his senior—the terrorist.

"Sure there's a way to be saved—just kill them before they kill you."

The young man who stood there had a presence completely different from the person he'd been a moment before.

The middle-aged conductor shuddered. It wasn't because he was afraid of the gun; no, it was because of the eyes of the man who had it trained on him. They weren't the eyes of the young man who'd been innocently telling ghost stories. They were eyes that swallowed everything—eyes that *destroyed* everything. Dark and deep, with a hard glitter to them.

Their color seemed to hold a mixture of hatred and pity and scorn, and it was all turned on him. Black flames, shining fiercely, as if all the light were turned toward the inside of his eyeballs… That was what his eyes were like. Just what sort of life did someone have to live to end up with eyes like those?

Even as the middle-aged conductor trembled at that thought, he realized they looked a lot like the eyes of his fanatical comrade, Chané.

However, frankly, that didn't matter one bit. Either way, if nothing changed, he was going to get killed. That alone was a fact he understood clearly.

"Wa-wait, please wait, *Claire*."

"No."

With that, the young conductor—Claire Stanfield—began to squeeze the gun's trigger.

He depressed it slowly, as if enjoying the time before he dealt death.

During that interval, there was enough time to run or counter-attack. However, Claire's eyes wouldn't allow it. It felt to the victim, though, that if he tried something like that, it would invite results more painful than death.

For just a moment, the finger paused.

"Oh, right. Here's the rest of my story. To keep the Rail Tracer from coming, you have to believe this story, and if he's already there, you have to get away from him until the sun rises... Although it's too late now."

The ingenuous way he'd talked up until a moment before was gone. He spoke dispassionately, in a tone that was rough and end-lessly cold, like blades of ice.

"The Rail Tracer will definitely appear for you people. This gun-shot will wake him. Your death will wake him."

He began to squeeze the trigger again. At that point, finally, the middle-aged conductor opened his mouth to scream. He raised his hands to resist.

...But it was all too late.

"Die, sacrifice."

A gunshot.

The sound traveled along the rails, echoing sharply...
Traveling far...
Very, very far away...

A spray of deep-crimson blood spattered over the wall in the narrow conductors' room.

In almost the same moment, the door opened.

*   *   *

"What the hell?"

When someone spoke behind Claire and he turned, a conductor was standing there, his eyes round.

He wore the special *Flying Pussyfoot* conductor's uniform, whose basic color was white.

"Who are you?" Claire asked the man. His face was expressionless.

There should only be two conductors on this train: me, and the guy I just killed... Come to think of it, what was this middle-aged conductor's name, anyway?

As he was thinking these things, the man in white waved both hands and said:

"Easy, easy, put that dangerous thing away, please. I'm not your enemy."

The man smiled brightly as he spoke. Quietly, Claire turned the gun on him.

"Like I could trust a guy who isn't panicking in a situation like this? Tell me who you are and what you want."

With that reasonable statement, he began to put pressure on the trigger.

"Wow. Busted already?"

Promptly changing his tone, the fake conductor warped his lips into a smirk. On seeing it, for some reason, Claire threw the gun to the floor.

The fake conductor watched this, looking mystified. Possibly because he hadn't yet made eye contact with Claire, his expression still held absolute confidence.

"What's the deal, huh?"

Confident wasn't quite the word for Claire's answer. It sounded more like a fragment of routine conversation.

"You seem like the type who wouldn't tell the truth if all I did was turn a gun on you, so I'm going to torture you a little."

Upon hearing that, the fake conductor burst out laughing.

"You're gonna *what*?! Torture, he says! What era are you from, huh?"

Ignoring the cackling man, Claire released the lock on the door that led to the outside. When he opened it, a cold wind blew in, searing its way into his body.

"C'mon, pal, what're you doing? I mean, I'm tickled you threw your piece away for me, but…"

Smirking, the fake conductor raised his voice, putting a hand into his jacket.

"Even if you're unarmed, I've got a gun— Huh?"

But Claire had vanished.

It had looked as if he'd walked right out the open door and fallen off the train, but that had to have been his imagination…right?

Drawing his weapon, the fake conductor slowly approached the door.

Leaning out slightly, he pointed the handgun to his left and right, but up ahead was the side of the train, and to the rear was a dark, receding landscape, and that was all.

Was he still inside, then? He hastily turned back around, and in that instant, something tremendously strong yanked the cuffs of his trousers backward.

"_____!"

In spite of himself, he pitched over, falling forward, but the force didn't ease up. It kept pulling the fake conductor out.

"Waugh, wah-wah-waaah-AAAaaaaAh!"

Even from his prone position, he managed to turn his head to look back, and then he saw something unbelievable.

The sleeves of the conductor's uniform had sprouted from below the open door, and their ends had latched onto his legs.

Th-the conductor? That's nuts! He's down there?! How—?!

As he was thinking this, his body was dragged outside all at once. The cold wind rushed past him, and he felt himself fall a short distance.

In the instant he thought, *I'm falling,* his body stopped with a jolt in midair.

The next thing the impersonator knew, Claire had him in a full nelson hold.

"??????—!"

The man was confused. He couldn't even imagine what was happening, or how.

Claire had his legs hooked around the metal fittings under the car and was holding the phony with his free-hanging upper half.

From this completely crazy position, he was gradually lowering the other man toward the ground.

In the midst of a roar that combined the sound of the moving train and the wind, Claire murmured in the man's ear:

"All right, I'm going to ask you again… Who are you?"

The fake conductor had regained enough presence of mind to be able to respond, but as a result, he refused to just tell him the answer. He began to struggle, trying to point the gun in his right hand behind him.

"Too bad."

The man's body lurched, tipping down, and his right arm made contact with the ground.

"Gaaaaaaaaaaaaaaaah!"

The shock and pain were far greater than what he'd imagined. He tried to raise his hand, but Claire was holding his arm, and he wouldn't let him up.

The gun in his right hand was knocked away in the blink of an eye…along with his hand, up to the wrist.

"Who are you?"

The question came again, but the man only screamed in pain.

Claire lowered his body, pressing his arm to the ground again.

By the time the fake conductor's right arm was gone up to the shoulder, Claire had gotten him to tell him everything about himself.

He said his name was Dune and that he was a member of the Russo Family. More accurately, he was a direct subordinate of Ladd Russo, and part of a faction that had broken off from the Russo Family that very day.

In addition, he told him Ladd's group was planning to hijack this train, kill half the passengers, and then crash the train into the station.

On reflex, Claire doubted their sanity, but apparently, sanity for this guy Ladd was the equivalent of insanity for ordinary people.

First, they'd throw the bodies of the passengers they'd killed onto the tracks; a "collector" who wasn't on the train would inform the railway company, and in the hours before the train arrived in New York, they'd squeeze as much money as possible out of the company.

Then they'd stop the train at a designated spot, meet up with the collector—who would arrive by car—and make their getaway. When they did, Ladd would probably kill all the passengers who'd seen their faces.

And, in order to take over the conductors' room, Dune had gone out of his way to wear a fake conductor's uniform.

"Why would you do that? It's pointless. If you just wanted to get control of the train, all you had to do was shoot us. There's no need to wear a uniform and pass yourself off as one of us."

As he answered Claire's question, Dune smiled; it was as if the prolonged exposure to extreme pain had fried the connections between his nerves.

However, what was truly worthy of disgust lay in what he said.

"Heh, heh-heh, heh. It's atmosphere, fella, atmosphere! Ladd loves games like that. Dressing like a conductor puts you in the right mood, and when I walk around the train later, the passengers will look at me with hope in their eyes. He says he likes killing 'em right after that—after their hope. I'm partial to it myself. Hee-hee, hee, hee-hee-hee-hee-hee…"

In response to the man's answer, Claire fell silent for a little while. Then, quietly, he spoke. The brutal color that had been in his eyes a moment ago was fading, and their former color was returning. However, those eyes seemed to hold a slight unease, and as Claire continued his interrogation, his expression clouded.

"How did you get those clothes so you could create this 'atmosphere' of yours? Those are *Flying Pussyfoot* exclusives. Only a few people have them."

"Hee, hee-hee. I picked 'em up at the station this morning! I got 'em from the conductor who got off this train when it pulled into Chicago and you got on! A pale guy with short hair!"

Tony. The face of the fellow conductor whose duties he'd taken over that afternoon rose in Claire's mind. He was a cheerful Italian conductor, and he'd taught Claire the ABCs of the job.

"What…did you do with him?"

"Hee-hee, he's probably feeding the rats in the Chicago sewers right about now!"

After blurting this out all at once, Dune realized it was something he should never have said.

The pain was keeping his brain from working, and he'd forgotten he was in a desperate situation.

"H-h-hang on, I lied!"

It was already too late. Claire's right hand was on the back of Dune's head. His eyes were filled with something even deadlier than before, and the bearing he'd worn, that of a conductor, had vanished completely.

With enormous strength stabilizing his head, Dune's body—along with Claire's upper body—was approaching the ground.

"Wa-wa-wait! You just killed a conductor yourself! What the hell are *you*?!"

Even at that protest, the force didn't let up. Claire only lowered his body slowly toward the ground. The afterimages made the gravel ballast look as if it was flowing like a river. At the speed this train was traveling at, if you scraped something against that gravel, it would turn into an excellent grater. He'd already proved this using Dune's arm.

In the interval before his nose touched the ground, Dune listened to Claire's long murmur:

"Me? I'm Claire Stanfield… Or 'Vino.' That might be easier for you mafia types to recognize."

Vino! I've heard of that! I've heard of him! He's a hitman who does jobs all around the States, and he picked up the nickname "Vino" because his kills are messy, and there's always a ton of blood left behind after he does a job. Who'd have thought he was really a conductor?!

No wonder he does jobs all over the place... But honestly, I couldn't care less about that, help me, let me go— Oh shit, shitshitshitshit—

"But it's different now."

Different whatever who cares just save me I'm begging you savgyaugalflaryuleuryeruru

rururururrrrrrrr

His face reached the ground, and in almost the same moment, Dune lost his sight, his consciousness, and his life.

Pulling the corpse back up, Claire tossed it into the middle of the conductors' room. His victim's blood had sprayed over him, dyeing his clothes bright red.

The corpse's head was twisted at an impossible angle, and its face and right arm had been completely ground off. The cut surfaces were extremely dirty and gruesome. If someone who didn't know any better saw this corpse, they'd probably think its face and arm had been chewed off...by some cruel, brutal monster far outside the realm of humanity.

Claire didn't try to wipe off the blood that had splashed over half his face. Instead, he used his fingers to draw red stripes below his eyes.

In a way, he might have meant it as a ritual, a prelude to what he was about to do.

Quietly, to himself, Claire murmured the rest of the words Dune hadn't been able to hear:

"—To you, I'm a monster. A monster who's going to devour all of you."

He looked up into empty space and grinned.

"Starting now, as far as you and this train are concerned—I'm the Rail Tracer."

BACC 19

THE GRAND PU

ANO!

3 1

NK RAILROAD

EXPRESS
THE MAN WHO WOULDN'T DIE

The dining car was filled with an amiable commotion.

Czes ran among the tables, chasing a girl who seemed to be close to his apparent age.

He and the girl were in the same first-class compartment on the train, and the girl had innocently suggested, "Let's explore the train together!" Czes hadn't been at all interested, but if he was going to act the part of "the boy the whole world liked," going along with her would probably be a sound move.

He'd thought things like that for more than two centuries, and in situations like this, he was able to naturally present himself as a child.

Following a girl whose name he didn't know, he ran to the middle of the dining car.

Come to think of it, I remember doing something like this when we crossed to this continent from Europe. I was the only child. When I said, "Let's explore the ship," I wonder who went with me. I just can't seem to remember... Well, it doesn't matter. Someday, when I "eat" them all, the answer will probably be lying around somewhere.

Czes had been thinking too many pointless things. His concentration was scattered, and his shoulder rammed into the back of a man who was sitting at the counter.

"*Mghk-ghk-gak!*"

The man seemed to have had his mouth full; the food had gotten stuck in his throat, and he was panicking.

When he looked, he saw it was the same tattooed guy he'd run into before boarding. Running into the exact same person: That was unlucky. Czes didn't feel particularly bad about it, but he decided to apologize immediately.

"Aah! Mister, again…! I'm really sorry!"

The guy had tears in his eyes, but even so, he forced a smile for Czes.

"Oh, no, it's okay. It's fine. I'm completely fine. What about you two? Are you all right?"

Czes nodded, smiling just the way he had earlier. For someone with a tattoo on his face, this man was a real soft touch. *A guy like this, all flash and no bang, will probably go his entire life without gaining anything.* That was what he was thinking, privately, but he didn't let any of it show in his expression.

After that, the girl's mother came up as well, and they started to make cheerful small talk.

Then a girl who wore glasses over an eyepatch looked at Czes and said:

"Is the little boy by himself?"

"Yes, he's—oh, good gracious. I haven't asked his name yet."

Ah yes, she's right.

Czes had decided to introduce himself to everyone by a pseudonym. He'd had to use his real name when reserving his train ticket, but when talking to ordinary people, he could give a false name without any trouble. It would be better to avoid having strangers know his real name as much as possible.

Having made this decision, Czes had settled on the pseudonym "Thomas." It was the name of Thomas Edison, the "King of Inventors," who'd died that year. He'd thought he wouldn't be likely to forget that one before they reached New York.

However.

"My name is Czeslaw Meyer—"

Giving that hard-to-pronounce name, Czes paused for a moment. During that short interval, his brain moved at dizzying speed.

What's going on?! I know I moved my mouth to say "Thomas" just now! It was almost as if my body refused to…

He remembered a similar situation. It had been back when *he* was still alive. At a market in town, someone had asked his name, and when he'd tried to give a false one on the spur of the moment, his mouth had blabbed his real name all on its own. At the time, *that guy* had been standing a short distance away, and he'd known that had been the cause, but…

The restraint the demon had given them. A price that was far too light for immortality:

Immortals will be unable to use false names with one another.

Right now, that restraint had informed him of a very important fact:

There is an immortal very close to me—

Czes was speechless, but it would do him no good to panic here. If the immortal hadn't noticed him yet, there was no sense in making himself stand out and attracting their attention.

He regained his composure and continued, saying something suitable. Except for giving a false name, he could tell any lie he wanted, so he made up a reasonable explanation for his journey.

"—Please call me Czes. I'm on my way to New York to see my family."

Next, the lady and the girl paid their respects as well.

However, Czes only registered their names; he was keeping his attention focused on the people in the dining car.

Thinking in terms of earshot, they were probably here in the dining car. That said, he didn't recognize any of the faces. He didn't see anyone who seemed to be in disguise, and the gunman and the girl with the eyepatch in front of him were more "in costume" than "disguised."

Who on earth is here? I can't see into the kitchen; could they be in there? Or else—

If possible, he wanted to deny the thought that came to him:

Is it another immortal entirely, someone who wasn't on that ship…?

As far as he was concerned, that was a truly terrifying idea. If there was an immortal other than the people who had been on board the ship, it would mean he no longer knew how many immortals were left, or what they looked like.

One day, a man he didn't know would walk up to him, smiling, and abruptly set his right hand on his head.

That was all it would take, and Czes's life would be absorbed and gone.

This was the one thing Czes couldn't allow. It wasn't the dying he minded. He thought he'd lived long enough already. The problem was that some third party would know about the distortion that had existed between *that guy* and himself. That would be the most unbearable humiliation there was. It was terror itself.

That was why Czes had chosen to live as he did now. Even if he had to view all others as prey, had to devour them all...he had to become the last immortal in the world.

If the other person was an immortal he didn't know, he needed to discover how they'd become immortal and how many others there were. The easiest way to learn would be to find and "eat" them.

In order to do that, it was essential for him to identify the other immortal. Should he stealthily wound them all, one by one, or go around setting his right hand on each person's head directly? But that would make it easy for the other person to spot him as well.

I absolutely have to get rid of the immortal here. No matter what it takes.

Even as Czes privately harbored these black thoughts, he made sure to keep his "innocent child" expression in place.

Just then, the man in the gunman costume turned to him and called out loudly:

"That's right. If you'd done something bad, the Rail Tracer would have eaten you already!"

"Chomp! Just like that!"

A gunman costume and a bright-red dress. A couple of passengers, a man and a woman, in eccentric outfits. He remembered their names had been Isaac and Miria, or something like that.

Isaac's voice had pulled Czes back to reality, and to calm his mind, for the moment, he decided to listen to his story.

"—That's how my old man used to threaten me, anyway."

"It frightened you, didn't it!"

"Huh? The R-Rail Tracer? Wh-what's that?" the tattooed guy asked timidly.

When he looked, the man's legs had begun to quietly shake.

"What, you don't know about it, Jacuzzi? You see, the Rail Tracer is…"

"…And so, if you tell this story on a train…it comes to that train, too. ——The Rail Tracer!"

"Eeeeeeeeeeeeek!"

"The Rail Tracer," huh? An absurd story. Although I suppose my own body and the demon are no different. When you look at it that way, that monster might really exist.

Even as he'd kept an eye on his surroundings, Czes had listened to Isaac's story.

If you do something bad, you get eaten, hmm? If that thing actually exists, I imagine I'll be the first one it eats. By the world's standards, I'd certainly fall into the "bad" category. In fact, even now, I'm about to sell a large quantity of explosives to the mafia.

If they used them in a dispute, there was bound to be damage to the general public as well.

"Damage" was an abstract way to phrase it: If the explosives in question were used in the middle of town, there would certainly be deaths. Absolutely. A large number of them. Czes was well aware of this, and he was going ahead with the transaction, anyway.

That wasn't all. Even before now, Czes had used his young appearance to trick and ensnare all sorts of people. Sometimes he'd done it to make his life easier. Sometimes he'd simply abandoned himself to his hatred of humans.

…So what? It isn't my problem.

To Czes, the question of how to eat the other immortals was far more important than the lives or deaths of strangers, or whether he was good or evil.

If it was for the sake of that hunger, he thought he wouldn't mind if everyone else in the world died.

Eternal loneliness would be far better than having that damnable knowledge absorbed by someone else.

As Czes thought this, his lips wore the faintest trace of a wry smile.

$$\Longleftrightarrow$$

Rachel, who was currently stealing a ride, was hiding on the train with astonishing boldness.

She sat at a table in the dining car and, with no hesitation, ordered food.

It wasn't as if she didn't have money, and she bore no grudge against the train's cooks. Consequently, she had no issue with paying for food. Besides, the dining room on this train was managed independently of the railway, which made it even less of a problem.

She hadn't been completely careless in entering the dining car, though. She'd taken her seat just after the conductor finished his first inspection, so she wouldn't need to worry about having her ticket checked for a while.

In addition, the dining car was shared by everyone from first class to third class. People wore a wide variety of clothing, and even her own outfit, which was very nearly work clothes, didn't seem blatantly out of place.

On top of that, when taking a seat, she'd strictly observed the rule of sitting by a window. Although she called it a "rule," it was just something she'd set for herself, so there was no penalty for violating it. However, if she was caught as a result, she wouldn't get away with a mere lecture.

That said, there's an awfully aggravating guy on this train…

She was looking at a man with a little mustache who was greedily devouring the finest item on the menu. He was an ugly man, not "portly" but just plain fat. He'd been boasting about himself nonstop for a while now, and his coarse laugh sent spittle flying.

"Wah-ha-ha! It's all thanks to my deep pockets that I'm able to ride high-class trains run by other companies!"

That wasn't what had irritated her, though. She'd recognized the man.

There was no way she could have forgotten him. He was an executive at the railway company where her father had worked. He was also the man who had framed her father while he personally remained at the company, bathed in comfort. From the way he was behaving, he still hadn't slipped out of his executive's chair. The sight of him threw a stagnant shadow across Rachel's heart.

She thought about punching him, but she knew there would be no point. In any case, since she was a fare-jumper, she couldn't risk causing a disturbance.

As she clenched her fists, the vulgar voice continued to ring out callously.

"Well, living a life of ease is my reward for having been faithful to the company and its people! Bwa-ha-ha-ha-ha-ha!"

Don't give me that "Bwa-ha-ha" crap. To hell with you. Get cursed and rot and fall into the ocean and get swarmed by wharf roaches and eaten down to the bone. I don't even want you coming back as scum on the waves. Disappear without a trace.

Biting back her anger, Rachel willed a curse on the whiskered pig, then made sure not to look in his direction again.

As she was eating the food that had been brought over from the counter (half in hopeless frustration), a young guy ran by her. He was crying.

He had a tattoo of a sword inked on his face, and at a glance, he looked a little like one of the pirates who haunted the Caribbean. However, his expression was scrunched up miserably, and veritable waterfalls of tears were streaming from his eyes.

In the instant the guy passed her, she heard him muttering in a low voice:

"The conductor, I need the conductor, fast…"

He's not planning on bringing the conductor back here, is he?

Rachel felt slightly uneasy, but she decided to continue her meal and keep an eye on the situation.

Before long, the door the tattooed guy had exited through opened, and a man in white appeared. Everything he wore was white, from his necktie to the toes of his shoes, and he looked like a country bumpkin who was going to be in a wedding.

In sharp contrast to the tattooed guy, this man strode grandly between the tables.

For just a moment, Rachel's eyes met his.

She looked away immediately, but she felt strangely unsettled. She couldn't seem to shake the feeling that he was sending out a danger signal, a type that was different from the orchestra couple she'd seen before boarding.

Focusing her most intense wariness on the man, she continued to keep tabs on the situation.

She had a bad feeling about this. A really bad feeling. It wasn't her instincts as a habitual ride-stealer. Her experience as an information broker's gofer, her dealings with a wide spectrum of underworld society—*those* were trying to tell her something.

In preparation for the time when she might need it, Rachel quietly began opening the window.

That time arrived almost immediately.

Inside the dining car, three yells went up.

Each voice carried well, and the words reached everyone in the car.

The men in black tuxedos, who'd come in through the forward door, yelled:

"Everyone on the ground!"

In their hands, they brandished machine guns.

The man in white, who'd been in the center of the dining car, yelled:

"Everybody reach for the sky!"

In his right hand, he held a shiny, copper-colored handgun.

The man in ragged clothes, who'd come in through the rear door, yelled:

"Hey, hey, hey! Nobody move!"

In his hand, he held a single fruit knife.

*　　*　　*

Dripping with cold sweat, the man next to Rachel muttered:
"Wha...what do you want us to do...?"

The men looked at one another's faces. All of them wore expressions that said, *What the heck is this?*

The first to move was the raggedy guy with the knife.

"Uh..."

Mumbling in a low voice, he took a couple of steps backward.

"Sorry to disturb you, folks."

He closed the door quietly, then ran off in a hurry.

One solitary knife hadn't been enough to balance the situation, but as a result, the three-way standoff collapsed.

...And that was the cue for tragedy.

The man in white immediately drew his gun and fired off three shots in rapid succession. The passengers all began to scream, cowering down and covering their heads.

Of the bullets the white suit fired, one made a direct hit on one of the black suits. Taking the bullet in the shoulder, he spun around and fell to the floor.

As if in response, a rain of lead erupted from the black suits' machine guns.

Their aim was accurate, and in the blink of an eye, the white suit's chest was dyed red.

While the passengers screamed, Rachel slowly stood up, opening the window as she did so.

As the man in white fell over backward, he fired several shots at the ceiling. Aim had nothing to do with it; the shock had only made his arm and fingers move.

Instantly, the machine guns roared again.

This time, a ferocious impact ran through the white suit's stomach, and his body bounded up in a V-shape.

Then the life faded from the man's eyes, and he slumped heavily to the floor.

By that time, Rachel had already slipped out of the train. Dexterously clinging to the ornamentation on the side of the car, she worked her way down, skillfully sliding through a gap between two of the wheels.

The passengers and black suits were all completely focused on the gun battle. The only one to witness Rachel's disappearance was the man who'd been sitting next to her.

⟺

After that, a terribly hyperactive friend of the white suit appeared and reversed the situation in a twinkling.

While the passengers were confused, unable to grasp the situation, one lone person did grasp it, quite calmly.

That lot... They may prove useful.

As Czes lay facedown in front of the counter, he was thinking about using the man in the white suit.

"All right, Czes. Please take care of Mary."

"Uh-huh!"

In response to Mrs. Beriam's voice, Czes nodded decisively, then took the girl's hand and left the dining car. He opened the door and started walking, looking around carefully as he went. At least for the moment, he didn't see any white suits in the corridor.

Leading Mary by the hand, he headed down the quiet corridor toward the rear cars. As far as Czes was concerned, this was a truly convenient situation.

After the attack, Mrs. Beriam had told him, "Czes, I want you to go hide somewhere with Mary." Personally, he'd wanted to leave the dining car and go find the white suits, but under the circumstances, if he'd said he was going out alone, the people around him would probably have stopped him.

In the midst of that situation, Mrs. Beriam, worried for her daughter, had given him a good excuse for going out. He couldn't possibly let it go unused.

Only, naturally, from this point on, Mary would get in the way. He could take her to the white suits and give her to them. He could also kill her here.

However, Czes really didn't feel like it. It wasn't because he felt sorry for her. The girl seemed to be about the age he looked. Deceiving her, betraying her... Wasn't that exactly what *that guy* had done to him?

He felt no guilt over killing children. If it was necessary, Czes wouldn't hesitate to use livers taken from living children in his research, but betrayal was something else entirely. The idea of doing something on par with the man he hated most set a ferocious self-loathing ablaze inside him.

He thought nothing of deceiving adults. That said, it wasn't that he viewed children as sacred. Over the past two hundred years, he'd seen far more than enough of the cruelty and ugliness in them. The reason he couldn't ensnare them, even so, was probably because he saw his own former self in the other child.

The girl held Czes's hand, trailing after him. Although her eyes were filled with fear, they didn't hold the slightest doubt about *him*. If her eyes *had* been suspicious, he would probably have been able to get rid of her here, but...

How much of a shackle will these damnable memories insist on being?!
Even as Czes fumed inwardly, his hand held Mary's tightly.

When they'd passed through the lead second-class carriage and were nearing the next one, he spotted a janitor's closet beside a bathroom.

Carefully, he opened the door. Inside were mops and buckets, stored neatly. If he pushed the mops over to a corner, there would probably be room for a child to hide.

"Okay, Mary, go in. You'll be able to hide in here, if you're on your own."

"B-but... Czes, what about you?"

Mary watched him with worried eyes.

"I'll go on ahead and see how things look, so you hide here, Mary. Whatever happens, don't move. It'll be fine. I'll be right back."

When Czes told her this, even though she was trembling, Mary nodded.

In fact, once he'd finished negotiating with the white suits, he did intend to come straight back. Depending on how his discussion with them went, he might end up putting her life in danger—which would once again amount to betrayal, so Czes wanted to avoid it no matter what.

Dammit, why am I hesitating? Every person in this world is prey, nothing more. They're just livestock. Wasn't that how I thought of them?

Calm down. You're only feeling sorry for her, that's all. Sometimes people feel guilty about killing lambs and eating their meat. This is no different.

Czes didn't consider that even negotiating with the white suits might be a betrayal in and of itself. He had promised he'd protect Mary, but the other people on the train were none of his concern.

That's right. In order to remind myself that I am something extraordinary, and to seal these damnable memories away, and, most of all, so that I can survive—this train must become a noble sacrifice.

Giving the very best smile he could manage, he quietly closed the door on the waiting girl.

Czes had forced that smile, and the tense muscles of his face wouldn't revert to his former expression easily.

Even though he should have been used to faking childlike smiles…

⇐⇒

"C'mon, somebody switch me for guard duty."

In the freight room, one of the black suits was making demands of the other two around him.

"Hey, don't just leave your post."

"Nobody cares. They won't cut those ropes that easily. And anyway, watching hostages isn't in our job description."

"There was no way around it. Somebody showed up."

Technically, their job was to keep an eye on the Lemures' weapons. The three of them had had too much time on their hands, but then, abruptly, the situation had gotten complicated.

They'd heard somebody running down the corridor, so they'd leveled their guns and gotten ready to go outside.

Then, before they could open the door, the door had opened on its own.

A weird thug had been standing there, and as they threatened him with their guns, a couple in white had come along as well. With no help for it, they had collared all three, only to have one last goon show up. They hadn't known what was going on, but for the moment, they'd captured them all, tied them up with ropes, and tossed them into the next freight room over...

"It's within the parameters of our orders. Our instructions were to grab anyone who spotted us. If you understand that, get back to your post."

"Yeah, and I'm *sayin'*, somebody switch with me."

"All right, all right. For now, let's go have a look at 'em."

With that, one of the black suits went out into the corridor with the other one.

The remaining suit called to their receding backs:

"Sure, and I'll use the wireless to tell Mr. Goose about them."

However, his comrades didn't respond.

"Hey, you could at least answer..."

He'd just stuck his head out the door and called to them when he realized there was something weird about the situation.

Two men had left for the next freight room, but only one was standing in the corridor.

"Hmm? Where'd George go?"

The man in the black suit and glasses asked about his missing comrade, but as before, there was no reply.

"Hey, what's the matter?!"

The comrade in the corridor was trembling violently. Finally, he managed to squeeze out a response:

"He... He's gone..."

"Huh?"

The man shook even harder; his back was to the window.

"He disappeared. I just, I turned around, and he was g—"

"Hey! Behind you!" the black suit shouted abruptly.

A monotonous row of windows lined the freight car corridor. One of them was wide open. It was the one right behind his comrade.

There was a red shadow in that window. It wasn't the reflection of something in the car—the window was open as far as it would go.

That red "something" was definitely *standing outside the train*.

Then that crimson streak reached for his comrade's back.

"Uh...?"

The man by the window didn't have time to turn around or even scream.

In a shockingly splendid motion, his body rose into the air. Then he was sucked out into the darkness, like water from a draining bathtub.

"Huh?"

The bespectacled black suit was confused.

It hasn't even been thirty seconds since my comrades went outside. How can they both have disappeared in thirty seconds? Not only that, but one of them vanished right in front of me. What the hell? How can I still not understand any of this? Am I really that dumb?

As he stood there, stunned, something red appeared at the edge of his vision once again.

A violent red, floating in the darkness. It was both terrifying and beautiful.

Slowly, the scarlet shadow disappeared behind the outside wall, and then only pitch-black darkness flowed quietly past the window.

At that point, the black suit with glasses finally managed to scream.

⇔

Claire hated his name.

He had no plans to change it, but as a guy, it irked him to be called by a girl's name.

He'd heard that he'd been named after his grandfather. It was true that, up until the first half of the nineteenth century, the name "Claire" had been used for boys as well. However, in this day and age, it was a name that got him mistaken for a girl no matter where he went.

He hated the name, but he held no grudge against his parents. In any case, there was no point in resenting people who were already dead.

If they'd been alive, he might have complained a bit, but they'd been dead for as long as he could remember.

After that, Claire had been raised by the Gandors, who'd lived in the next apartment over.

Old man Gandor had been the boss of a mafia family so small that a good gust of wind could have taken it out. Among the syndicates of New York, it was on a level with the lowest organization's pet dog.

When old man Gandor had died, Claire had been picked up by the circus. He'd thought being able to touch your own head to your butt and do one-handed handstands was normal, but apparently, it was something pretty amazing. The circus folk had said stuff about hereditary musculature and build, but Claire couldn't have cared less.

If there was one thing he hadn't liked, it was that afterward, no matter how hard he'd trained and mastered techniques, the people around him had explained it all away with the word *talent*. It was humiliating, as if his effort was being reduced to nothing, but in the end, he'd accepted that, too. *I bet mastering techniques this simple doesn't count as "effort,"* he'd thought. In which case, he decided, he'd acquire something even bigger than his so-called talent.

The bottom line was that his efforts still hadn't been acknowledged by anybody. It was true that he'd put in twice as much effort as anyone else, but to ordinary people, his abilities hadn't seemed like the sort of thing "effort" could have any effect on.

Claire had thought he'd send the money he earned at the circus to the Gandor brothers, who were just like family to him, but the world wasn't that kind. It wasn't that he hadn't managed to earn any money. By the time he'd started to earn at a certain level, the three brothers had greatly expanded their territory. To other organizations, they still looked weak, but their revenue had already grown far beyond his.

The circus troupe disbanded, and he was turned out into the world to fend for himself. Eventually, after many twists and turns, Claire had become a professional hitman. Freelance hitmen were quite rare, but he was getting along pretty well. There was a reason he'd quit circuses and used the job of conductor as his cover. In this profession, he moved far more frequently than circuses did, and he got to travel between major cities. For a freelance hitman, nothing could have been more convenient.

His kills were messy. Claire was fully aware of this. It was a bad habit of his: Unless he destroyed the target's body to a certain extent, he couldn't really relax. He thought their heart might not have stopped yet. It wasn't that he was a coward. His actions were based on the idea that if he was going to accept a contract to kill, it was good form to make sure the target was thoroughly dead.

Although this habit should have been a weakness, it had actually made him famous. This method of killing, which left abnormal puddles of blood at the scene, struck enormous terror into the hearts of other organizations.

At some point, Claire had picked up the nickname "Vino" (although he'd always worked under a pseudonym, anyway), and before he knew it, that name had permeated every major city. He was rumored to be an elusive monster who turned up in cities all across the States, and the alias "Vino" echoed quietly and deeply through underworld society.

I'm a conductor on the transcontinental railroad, so it's only natural that I'd show up in most major cities. And the idea of calling a guy who's built as thin as I am a monster... What do they call the middle Gandor brother, then? A demon? He's as big as two of me.

As he remembered the "family" he'd be meeting tomorrow, Claire's heart naturally settled down.

Even though he'd gotten pretty famous, the Gandor brothers

hadn't invited Claire to join their organization. That said, they didn't keep him at a distance, either, and they didn't try to make him stop working as a hitman.

While there were issues with that action as far as their humanity was concerned, it made Claire happy, and if it was for the Gandors, he took jobs at bargain rates. To be honest, he wouldn't have minded working for free, but they wouldn't let him do that.

And now he was on his way to meet them, in order to do his duty by them. From what he'd heard, the Gandor Family was currently at war with the Runorata Family, a syndicate that counted as one of the big guys, even in New York. He probably wouldn't be returning to his conductor job for the time being. He'd already told the rail company that after the train arrived in New York tomorrow, he'd be going on leave for a while.

The only remaining problem was whether this train would make it safely to New York.

He couldn't let the train stop.

They might keep chipping away at the Gandor Family because his arrival had been delayed. This was something he wanted to avoid at all costs.

If either the white suits or the black suits took over the train, its chances of arriving safely would shrink dramatically. Even if it reached New York, they'd probably find themselves in a standoff with the police. Besides, if they ended up fighting with the cops, some of the passengers were bound to get killed.

I won't give this train to those lowlifes. I won't let them kill the passengers, either, and I won't let them be used as hostages.

When he'd thought that far, Claire realized that partway through, he'd set the Gandors' matter aside and was genuinely worried about the passengers.

What's that about?

He examined his own heart.

I guess I liked being a conductor quite a lot, too.

In the moonlight, he smiled bashfully.

…Smiled bashfully as he clung to the side of the freight car with one hand, holding the corpse of a black suit with a broken neck under his arm.

⟺

Rachel had been traveling underneath the cars. She made her way through the gaps between the metal fittings like a monkey, heading for the rear of the train with what would have looked to the average person like extraordinary speed.

She was headed for the freight room. She didn't know what was going down, but she knew people from the orchestra had burst into the dining car with machine guns.

In that case, what about the man who was guarding their belongings in the freight room? If being an orchestra was a front, the man in the freight room was probably one of them, regardless of what they really were. In order to get a handle on the situation on this train as quickly as possible, Rachel had begun to move. Although she could have just sat quietly, she was intentionally heading into danger.

It was probably something like an occupational disease for information brokers. This was how she excused her curiosity to herself, although, technically, she was only a gofer.

When Rachel reached the area under the freight room, she leaned out between the wheels to look at the door on the side of the train. She didn't expect it to be open, but she wanted to find out anything she could about the state of the inside.

However, at that point, something unexpected happened.

The side door *was* open.

Ordinarily, that door should have been opened only when the train was stopped, in order to load or unload cargo.

The fact that it was open now meant there really was some sort of big incident going on…

At that point, Rachel's head stopped working for a moment. She'd noticed it: Beside the open door, a bright-red figure squirmed.

Since it was dark, and since she'd been focusing on the open door, at first she hadn't registered its presence. However, when she saw the thing beside the door, she understood the situation.

The door wasn't *open*. It was *being opened*, in the present progressive tense...at this very moment. By the red figure.

The red shadow didn't seem to have noticed her. It was clinging to the projections on the side of the train, in an astonishingly secure pose.

Before long, the door was fully open, and the thing went into the freight room as if nothing had happened.

For a moment, Rachel was dumbfounded, but the male screams she could hear mixed in with the noise of the train yanked her mind back to reality.

"Stop...... Stay back...... Stop, stop, *stooooooooop!*"

After an uncommonly frightened scream, a roar echoed in the freight car. However, it ended almost immediately. Assailed by a vague, bad premonition, Rachel began to draw her upper body back under the car.

But she was just a little too late.

Suddenly, the red shadow descended right beside her—actually, rather than "descended," it was like it dropped down from the opening in the side.

Then something even more problematic happened.

She made eye contact.

With the red shadow, the monster...

Claire had a slight problem.

He'd already disposed of two of the black suits who'd been guarding the freight room.

However, the third one had seen him drag the second one outside. Sure enough, that third one had used the transmitter and begun to contact his companions.

The lock on the door of this freight room was broken. He'd known this, and he'd decided to sneak in and finish him off.

By the time the guy screamed, it was too late. Claire caught his arm and raised it, and the man squeezed the trigger of his tommy gun in vain.

The machine gun had been pointed up. Naturally, not a single bullet hit Claire. When he twisted a little, the black suit let the gun fall with astonishing ease.

After that, he only had to drag him outside in the usual way and kill him by holding him against the ground. Holding a grown man in a head lock, Claire leaped out through the door with the air of a man walking down stairs.

Then he needed to stop by skillfully hooking his legs around the metal fittings. Anyone else would probably have fallen, or their legs would have been unable to take the strain and broken, or they would have gotten snarled in the wheels, and that would've been that.

However, he'd be fine. His expression was filled with self-confidence, and he actually had managed to do it, when—

At that point, unusually, a troubled expression appeared on his face.

Who's she?

Beside him, a woman's head protruded from a gap between the fittings under the train. He'd never seen her before. Was she one of the black suits or white suits?

As he hesitated, the man he held abruptly got heavier. Then, in the next instant, he got lighter.

When he looked, the black suit's legs were gone. Apparently, while he'd been kicking and struggling, they'd gotten caught in the wheels.

He must have been pulled with quite a lot of force, but Claire had maintained the full nelson without any trouble at all. As a result, the black suit's lower half had been ripped off. The man seemed to have lost consciousness before he even had time to scream. The shock of the pain might actually have killed him already.

Either way, he wouldn't be able to escape death by blood loss.

Well, no help for it.

For now, Claire flexed his legs and his back, pushing himself up. Using the recoil, he flung the top half of the black suit into the car.

Possibly, he'd used too much force: The man's ruined upper body hit the ceiling, then slammed to the floor.

Without paying any particular attention to this, Claire returned his gaze to the woman's head.

From the glimpses of clothing that was visible between the pipes, she didn't seem to be either a white suit or a black suit. And actually, he hadn't seen a woman like this when he'd been checking the passenger list. In that case, there was only one thing he could think of.

In spite of himself, Claire's conductor nature led him to ask the usual question.

For just a moment, the murderous intent left his eyes, and the conductor's bearing, the one he'd worn before the incident, returned.

That said, Rachel didn't have the wherewithal to notice a difference like that.

What? What's going on? What is this?!
Rachel was confused. Moving in a way that was clearly inhuman, the red shadow had ripped off the black suit's legs. Not only that, but he'd done it using the cruelest method imaginable: by tangling them in the train's wheels. In the moment when the black suit's legs got caught in the wheels, the entire car had lurched. Even though the impact had been that great, the red monster hadn't so much as flinched... Although he was holding on with only his legs, which he'd hooked around the pipes.

Throwing the corpse back into the car with one of those inhuman motions, the red shadow turned its eyes on Rachel.

Rachel couldn't move a muscle. She gazed quietly back into those eyes. Outwardly, she seemed calm, but on the inside, she was so scared she couldn't stand it. She just couldn't think of that red shadow's eyes as human. She'd looked at them for only a few seconds, and she still felt nauseated. It felt as if she were looking into a terribly deep hole. As if she were about to be pulled into that hole and killed.

Immediately afterward, the bloodlust in the monster's eyes faded, but Rachel wasn't in any shape to notice something like that.

The monster in front of her quietly opened its mouth—and said what were, in a way, the words Rachel feared most.

*   *   *

"May I see your ticket?"

"NOOOOOOOOOOOOOOOOOOOO!"
Rachel zipped back under the car like a snail's eye, then began to flee under the train, as fast as if she were running. Her arms and legs moved as if each were a separate living thing, wriggling and tangling with one another, carrying her torso away toward the front of the train.

What?! The conductor? Are you telling me that monster is the conductor?! No way! That's completely nuts! —But what other explanation is there? Why? Why is that thing talking like a conductor? I'm gonna die. If that thing nabs me for ride-stealing, it'll kill me for sure!

She'd infiltrated mafia hideouts to get information, but a terror she'd never experienced before ruled her body now. Its control kept her arms and legs moving, trying to get her as far from the monster as possible.

In that moment, she even considered jumping off the train.

The life returned to Claire's eyes, and his conductor persona burned with anger.

Why that little— So she is stealing a ride, huh? What am I going to do about that woman? Should I toss her off the train? Or should I make it so she can't stand up, hang a card that says "I steal rides" around her neck, and put her on display in the station?

For a moment, he considered going after her, but his hitman's sense checked him.

Whoops. I'm not a conductor now. I'm just a monster. I forgot.

As he casually thought better of it, the hitman's deadly expression returned to his face.

He leaped back into the freight room without any trouble, then began walking around, observing the condition of the room.

As he did, he noticed a machine of some sort, sitting on a large box. It seemed to be a wireless set, but it looked quite a bit smaller than the ones currently in use. Apparently, the enemy wasn't just a group of adrenaline junkies.

However, as far as Claire was concerned, that didn't matter. No matter what sort of enemy they were or how many people they had or what kind of traps were waiting for him, his self-confidence was big enough to destroy it all, and he knew he had the power to do it.

He picked up a few ropes that had been left in the freight room. They probably belonged to the black suits, but he might be able to use them for something. Claire wound the long rope around his waist and put the thin, short rope inside his coat.

Then he went on the attack again, looking for another target to destroy.

He was just a man cloaked in violence, protecting the peace of the train.

⟺

Ladd and Lua had just come from their first contact with Jacuzzi's group. Trailing another companion, the pair—the key figures of the group of white suits—entered the conductors' room.

To be completely accurate, the only one who actually stepped into the room was Ladd.

"This is straight-up weird. I straight-up don't believe this. What's with the ocean of blood? Ain't this weird? Actually, ain't it awesome? Whaddaya have to do to leave a mess like this after a kill, and how?"

Lua and the other white suit were at the entrance to the room, and they made no move to go inside. The entire floor was awash in blood, and a corpse with no face and a missing arm lay in the middle of it. Not only that, but the older conductor lay against the inner wall, with the back of his head blown off. That one had probably been shot to death.

"Hey, hey, hey, look, this fella with no face, ain't this him? Ain't it Dune? Hell, man, lookit that. That's what I call trying to steal a mummy and getting turned into one instead! And say, who killed Dune? How am I supposed to avenge him if I dunno who did it? Aah, aah, aah, Dune, poor bastard! His pals can't even avenge him!"

In contrast to the white suit outside the door, who had turned pale and averted his eyes, Ladd was acting genuinely wired.

As he imagined just what kind of monster had killed Dune, he jumped around as if he was really enjoying himself. Each time his feet came down, blood splashed up, and Ladd's white suit grew redder and redder.

Finally, Ladd gave a great laugh—"Hya-ha-ha-ha-ha-ha-ha-ha-ha-ha-ha-ha-ha-ha-ha-ha-ha-ha-ha-ha-ha-ha-ha-ha-ha-ha-ha-ha-ha-ha-ha-ha-ha-ha-ha-ha-ha-ha-ha-ha-ha-ha-ha-ha-ha-ha-ha-ha-ha-ha-ha-ha-ha-ha-ha-ha-ha-ha-ha-ha-ha-ha-ha-ha!"—then abruptly shut his mouth and left the conductors' room.

As he passed Lua, he spoke to her, his expression serious:

"Be careful. I dunno what it is, but something on this train is real bad news. Nobody sane kills things *that* dead. He's not some corpse-loving pervert like Bluebeard or a bloodthirsty killer like me, though. He's a monster with an overkill mania."

He stopped, glancing at Lua's face.

"I'm off to kill that guy and the black suits, so you go hide somewhere, a'ight?"

Ladd smiled. Unlike his earlier smiles, this one had warmth in it somewhere. Lua nodded. In response, his face warped again, and he said:

"I'm the one who's gonna kill you, see."

At those words, Lua blushed and nodded again.

The guy's a nutcase, as usual.

Their white-suited companion, who'd been watching the exchange, muttered this to himself, silently:

That line right there? That's what the rival in Westerns and stuff always says to the hero when he saves him. I've never heard anybody say it to their girlfriend or fiancée.

And he knew. He knew the guy had meant what he said and that someday, he probably would kill Lua.

He also knew that was what Lua wanted, too.

⟺

That's pretty horrendous. What happened here?

When he saw the legless corpse lying in the first freight room, Czes involuntarily sucked in his breath.

No matter how you looked at it, this couldn't be the work of the black suits. In fact, the dead man *was* a black suit. The next thing Czes thought of was the group in white suits: *If it was that lunatic who came to the dining car, then maybe…* The immortal was a possibility as well, but it wasn't as though immortals' physical strength changed very much; they just didn't die anymore. They had fewer weak points than the sort of vampire that turned up in novels, but in an ordinary fight, they'd definitely lose. That was immortals for you: They simply didn't die, and that was all.

In terms of other people who could have made this corpse…

Words Czes had heard just a moment ago surfaced in his mind.

The Rail Tracer.

"Yeah, right."

In spite of himself, Czes spoke this denial aloud. Maybe, somewhere deep in his heart, he was uneasy, and he'd tried to cancel it out by force.

Another possibility is that he took a direct hit from my explosives.

The thought reminded him of the hidden cargo he'd loaded on board. The explosives he was going to sell to the Runorata Family were being carried in the next car back. Half of it was powder explosives, packed in special boxes. The other half had been fashioned into clay grenades and sticks of dynamite. They were a bit like handicrafts he'd made for fun, but he'd heard that they actually did use clay bombs in Japan.

The Runorata Family was in the middle of a war, and they wanted explosives they could use immediately. They also wanted them to be powerful articles that were easy to handle.

This new type of explosive, which had been created as a by-product of Czes's research, was more powerful than conventional explosives, and its stability with regard to impacts had been improved. However, after all, it was just a research by-product. He'd been attempting to sell it off cheaply when the Runorata Family had bought it.

It wouldn't have been odd for anyone sent flying by those explosives to lose a leg or two, or even be blown away entirely, depending on the situation. That said, since there were no wounds on the corpse other than its missing lower half, he could eliminate that possibility easily.

So was it the white suits who'd killed this black suit after all, then?

In any case, he'd find out when he actually met them. Losing interest in the corpse, Czes started toward the conductors' room again. He'd almost run into some white suits on his way here, but their crazy leader-type hadn't been with them, so he'd ducked into nearby compartments or bathrooms and hidden until they passed by. After all, if he didn't negotiate with the group's central figure, he'd never get anywhere.

That man isn't the type to stay in one place. If I make for the conductors' room, I'm sure to find him at some point.

Half-convinced of this, Czes headed for the conductors' room.

And, as he'd planned, in the second freight car, he finally managed to run into Ladd.

"Nn?"

For now, Ladd and the others had decided to head back to the front of the train, but in the second freight car, they encountered a small figure.

It was the boy he'd seen in the dining car.

"What, kid? Need something?"

Ladd treated him coldly, but inwardly, he was already starting to want to kill the boy.

What's with you, brat? I know you were in that dining car a minute ago. I know you saw me slaughter that black suit, so what's with that face, huh? What are you so relaxed for? You think you're not gonna get offed because you're a kid? Don't mess with me, punk. I'll kill you.

As dark flames blazed inside him, the boy spoke, smiling brightly: "Mister, you're really strong, aren't you! You startled me!"

His intent-to-kill gauge fell slightly.

"Oh yeah? You think so?"

"Uh-huh! If you got into the ring, mister, they'd have put a belt on you by now, absolutely!"

The intent-to-kill gauge fell farther.

"Huh. I don't hate brats who are good at complimenting people. So? Whaddaya need?"

"Actually, I had a favor to ask you."

"A *favor*?"

The intent-to-kill gauge rose a bit.

"This isn't really the place for it. Let's step into this room to talk."

Saying this, the boy went into the freight room, then beckoned to him.

The intent-to-kill gauge rose.

"Hey, hey, hey, hey, you rotten little way-too-amiable brat. Do you know what we are?"

"Don't look so scary, mister."

The room held boxes of all different sizes; Czes found one that was just the right height and sat down on it.

"Can it. The only reason you've still got a pulse is that the great Ladd here is gonna be twenty-five this year and you didn't talk to me like I'm old. That achievement's all that's keeping you alive, and don't you forget it. Whether your 'favor' makes me laugh or ticks me off is gonna determine how much your life is worth, kid."

Ladd's lips were smiling, but his eyes were almost saturated with murderous intent.

However, without seeming the least bit daunted, the boy looked Ladd full in the face and innocently asked his "favor":

"Listen, mister, listen. All those people in the dining car—could you massacre them for me?"

Ladd's intent-to-kill gauge jumped and dipped violently.

His unsettled expression didn't escape the boy; he kept talking, pressing him harder.

Both his tone and his attitude had changed completely.

"You'll receive fair compensation, of course. You'll get to enjoy yourselves, and I'll be purchasing my own safety... Although I'll have to ask you not to pry into what I mean by 'safety' in this case."

On hearing what the boy said, Ladd's eyebrows came together, and the eyes of the other two opened wide.

Had those words actually come from this boy?

Of the group, Ladd was the first and only one to recognize his true nature, and he spoke.

"You...ain't no kid."

"You're quick on the uptake. That's a great help."

Nodding with a genial smile, Czes continued his negotiation.

"If you kill all the passengers, your reward will be two hundred thousand dollars."

Czes was getting five hundred thousand from the Runorata Family for the explosives. Viewed in that light, his offer to the white suit wasn't an unaffordable sum, and it would be a small price to pay if it let him identify the immortal. Once these guys killed the passengers, he could take his time eating the one who started to regenerate.

Considering that low-ranking workers in bootleg liquor factories were currently paid around two hundred dollars a week, it certainly was a huge sum... That said, this was contrasted by the fact that it just about equaled the amount Al Capone made from bootleg liquor in a day.

"Nah, I'm not touching that one."

Ladd was impressive, too: Immediately adapting to this abnormal situation—in which the other guy was an adult who looked like a kid—he promptly switched his brain over to financial negotiations.

"Just how many people do you think we'd have to kill in the dining car alone? Well, we could kill 'em easy, and we were planning on killing half of 'em, anyway, but I'm not letting you yank us around for chump change like that. Besides, we've already got a cash cow to milk. Right about now, my guy on the outside is threatening and sweet-talking the railway company out of about a million dollars. I'm just letting him do what he wants, so he might be asking for a billion or so."

"And you actually think a plan that reckless is going to work?"

"It's not a question of whether it will or not. It's all about guts. And hey, if you're gonna take that angle, there's no guarantee you'd pay up, either."

At Ladd's words, Czes's young face warped into a wry smile.

"That's very true. From what I can see, though, you may be a homicidal maniac, but you're ordinary enough to adjust to society, and amusingly, you even have subordinates. That said, you don't seem to plan at all. I'd assume you've lived this long by shrewdly responding to situations as they develop, correct?"

"Don't just decide how guys live…"

In contrast to Ladd, whose tension had begun to drop, Czes's words picked up momentum:

"In that case, shall I cooperate with you? I'm in the middle of a deal with New York's Runorata Family. After this incident is over, I wouldn't mind putting in a good word for you and ensuring that you're given a warm welcome."

On hearing that, the white suit behind Ladd raised an objection:

"The Runoratas are one of the biggest syndicates in New York. I doubt they'd agree to harbor mass serial killers that easily."

"That's simple. Just make it unnecessary for them to harbor you."

"Huh?"

"I've loaded a large quantity of explosives onto this train…for use in my transaction with the Runoratas, you see. After you've disposed of the people in the dining car, I'll detonate some of them. I brought extra, just in case, so that won't be a problem."

"What're you talking about?"

"We'll use that explosion to make them stop the train, and during that time, we'll disembark and make our escape. Ah, I'll need you to help carry the remaining explosives. In any case, the cause of the explosion will be simple: The mysterious group in black that occupied the train blew it up. It's sure to be front-page news."

Chuckling, Czes went on, his eyes gradually filling with madness. He wasn't aware of it, and he probably would have denied it, but his eyes were the same color as those of the man he'd once eaten.

The warped, stagnant color they'd been when he'd abused Czes.

"But listen—"

"It's fine. The station employees saw the 'orchestra' load a lot of cargo onto this train. Besides, those crates actually do seem to have been packed with lots of weapons. Everyone who's seen your faces will die, and you, who are on the passenger list, got caught up in the explosion and blown to kingdom come… What do you say to that?"

Then he struck his hands together lightly.

"Or, if you like, you could leave one member on the train and have them act as a 'survivor' and fabricate testimony."

When he'd said that much, Czes stopped to wait for the other man's reaction. After a short silence, Ladd spoke quietly:

"That don't make sense."

"Oh?"

"If you've got a bomb like that, why aren't you doing this yourself? Just light the thing, and you'd be done."

"That would be inconvenient for me... I've got business with a certain corpse, you see. If it got blown to bits, I'd have a problem."

Ordinarily, immortals regenerated around their brains. If he blew this one up with a bomb and their head happened to fly off the train, it would be a catastrophe. Besides, if the corpses were very fragmented and mixed together, the immortal might regain consciousness while he was searching for the regenerating body. Czes wanted to make finding the immortal for certain his top priority.

To finish up, Czes changed his tone and expression back to their childlike versions and asked his "favor" of Ladd:

"Please, mister... You'll do it, won't you?"

Intent-to-kill gauge at max.

Immediately, Ladd's "live eyes"—which brimmed over with energy—returned, and he cheerfully pointed his gun at Czes's forehead.

"You said I lived this long by 'shrewdly responding to situations' on the fly. Wrong, lousy brat. I've never once calculated how I live."

The next instant, Ladd's rifle spit fire, and the top half of the boy's head was blown off.

"I calculate how I kill."

⇔

"Why'd you kill him, Ladd? That would've been a pretty good deal."

"Mm, yeah. But did you see the guy's eyes? He had this look on his face that said 'I'm not gonna get killed.' He was sure we wouldn't kill him! He was making a monkey of the great Ladd Russo, see? It was sort of, y'know, frankly, he made me sick, so I shot him up."

"Yeah, but, c'mon…"

"I don't like it, though. Even right when I blew his head off, he looked cool as a cucumber… What the hell was that about?"

When Czes opened his eyes, Ladd and the others were no longer in the room.

…Good grief. That fellow's a trickier customer than I thought he would be. How many seconds was I unconscious? It's usually about twenty…

Czes's immortal body was apparently quite used to having its head destroyed. He'd regained consciousness at almost the same moment as he finished regenerating.

Huhn. He destroyed my head rather frequently, after all. With blunt instruments, knives, the wall, the floor… Come to think of it, that was the first time I've been shot with a gun. It's rather nice to have the pain be over in a moment like that.

After checking to make sure the wound in his head had closed completely, Czes started to leave the freight room.

Just then—

"Waaaaaugh! Jacuzzi! Stay with me! It's just a flesh wound!"

"Your wound is going to be just fine!"

There were voices yelling in the corridor, coming closer. They belonged to the weird gunman couple, Isaac and Miria.

Thinking it would be a bad idea to be seen here, Czes hastily hid behind a mountain of cargo.

"Huh? There's nobody here."

"Yes, it's deserted!"

Isaac and Miria began to search behind the cargo. Timing his move for when they got close to where he was, Czes circled around to the opposite side, careful not to make a sound.

"That's strange. From the way they were talking, it sounded as though somebody had been shot dead in here."

"Yes, like someone had brought up some sort of deal, and they'd turned them down and killed them!"

Why do they know all that?

Even as he wondered, Czes used the moment when Isaac and Miria had gone around behind the cargo to escape from the room.

There's no help for it. I'll just keep an eye on the situation for a while longer. After all, the group in black may get a chance to kill the hostages in the dining car.

⇔

Czes hadn't noticed, but…another figure had been lurking in that room.

The figure was dyed as red as wine.

I completely failed to pick up on that. Who'd have thought that Czes kid was full of such evil ideas? Or, no, I guess he isn't a kid.

Claire had been in charge of the passenger list, so he was able to put names and faces together for most people… Although the white suits and black suits all seemed to have used pseudonyms.

He'd happened to see the group of white suits go into this freight room, so he'd sneaked in from underneath. Each car on this train had a section of floor that could be opened for use during emergency inspections.

…And so he'd opened the trapdoor in the corner of the freight room, but he'd never expected to hear a conversation like that one. At the sound of the voices belonging to Isaac and Miria, Claire went back down under the train, quietly closing the trapdoor.

All right, what next? Well, Czes is dead, so let's call that good. I guess I'll just take things in order and go to the second-class compartment the white suits were in.

Claire, who'd been in the shadows of the cargo the whole time, was positive Czes had been shot and killed.

Prior to this point, Claire had disposed of two white suits in a third-class compartment. Because he hadn't felt like taking any extra trouble, he'd just tossed them out of the train, along with the corpses of three black suits that had been in the same room.

He'd had a reason for temporarily returning to the rear cars. Unless he sent the signal from the conductors' room at the designated times, the engineers would realize that something was wrong and stop the train. If that happened, the black suits and white suits might fly into a rage and start killing passengers. Even without that, if the train stopped, it would cause problems for Claire personally.

It was possible that the black suits had already taken control of the locomotive. However, since they'd gone to the trouble of having a treacherous conductor present, they were probably trying to operate the train as normally as possible. The black suits might not even have realized that the middle-aged conductor was dead.

Having drawn that conclusion, Claire had decided to make sure he kept sending the signal.

This meant he had to return to the conductors' room at set intervals.

On the way, he'd spotted the white suits and Czes and had followed them, and that had created the current situation.

Whoops. Crap, not good. The signal to the locomotive comes first.

Realizing what he needed to do next, he spun to face the other way under the train.

Fortunately, he still had some time left. He decided to check for remaining black suits as he went.

⟺

"See? Awesome, ain't it? Walking on the roof feels great, don't it?"

"…It's cold…" Lua murmured her response in a small, trembling voice.

Having heard about the roof from the gray magician, Ladd had wasted no time in climbing up, and then, imagine that: The stars were pretty, and he wouldn't be seen by any enemies who were walking through the train. Talk about bagging two birds with one stone.

On that thought, he'd had Lua and the other guy climb up as well, but apparently, the reviews weren't good.

"Man. How can you jump around like that in a dicey place like this?"

Ladd was bounding around as if it was nothing, but apparently, it was all the other two could do just to stand up.

"Really? You guys have lousy balance. You better eat a more balanced diet. Not that I know much about it."

Sounding disappointed, Ladd kept moving forward.

Then he spotted human figures several cars ahead. He couldn't tell what kind of people they were, but they seemed to be crawling over the roof.

Ladd's eyes shone as if he were a little kid with a new toy, and he schemed to find out who they were.

"Hey, I'm gonna head up to the first-class cars for a bit, so you guys, y'know, go back to the room and rest up."

Without waiting for the other two to respond, Ladd ran away over the roof. The fact that he managed to make almost no noise as he did so was pretty spectacular.

Lua and the other guy looked at each other, then climbed down at the coupling that was closest to their compartment. They weren't the least bit worried. They couldn't even imagine Ladd losing to a group of black-suit nobodies.

⇔

Chané stood.

Up on the roof of a first-class carriage, with the freezing wind at her back.

After picking off one of the white suits, she'd decided to go up on the roof and keep an eye on things for a while. They'd set guards in the dining car, and in that one car, the corridor and the room were combined.

That meant that, with their disadvantage in numbers, there was a large possibility that the white suits would cross the roof and launch a surprise attack.

Chané was planning to slaughter those white suits all by herself.

She wouldn't accept help from Goose or the others. She knew they'd betray her someday, too. Just as Nader had.

Goose's group was only after one thing: They wanted bodies like Huey's. What separated them from Nader was that they supported the revolution. However, to Goose and the others, Huey wasn't at its center. As soon as the revolution succeeded, as far as they were concerned, Huey would probably be in the way. They kept up the appearance of loyalty merely because they wanted to receive the "blessing" he said he'd give them. The blessing of having their bodies made like his.

Once they acquired those bodies, they probably intended to exile Huey. Yes, Goose and the others were under the impression that they had deceived Huey and were using him. What a pack of fools.

They had no idea that they were the ones being deceived.

Huey often told Chané—and only Chané—the truth. He probably understood that she'd follow him to the very end.

She knew: Huey Laforet's body was immortal.

He had recruited revolutionaries by saying he'd share that immortality.

But Huey couldn't actually share his immortality with others.

He wasn't actually interested in the world after the revolution.

What he wanted was to gauge the social limits of immortals.

Because Huey only wanted to see whether an immortal could win against a nation.

She also knew: Huey was kind enough to say he loved her.

It wasn't as a lover, though. Not at all.

Huey was her father.

And that, therefore, immortality wasn't genetic.

Very soon, her body would age past her father's.

She would most certainly die before he did.

If Goose's group rescued Huey, they would probably try to wrest immortality from him by force. That said, it was more dangerous for him to be the nation's prisoner. She'd heard there was an immortal in the upper echelons of the Bureau of Investigation. That man might "eat" her father.

There was only one person who knew her past.
Only one person who was her family.
Only one person who loved her.
Only one person she loved.
Huey Laforet.
She couldn't let him be stolen. She couldn't give him to anybody.

Chané intended to rescue Huey. She knew her father wouldn't be happy with this method—with taking hostages—but it didn't matter. She had said she was doing this for his sake, but it was really for the sake of her own desires, and nothing more.
She wouldn't let anyone get in the way, no matter who they were.
Not even a legendary monster.

There were two figures crawling toward her, over the dining car. They didn't seem to be white suits, but if they were planning to interfere, she'd show them no mercy. They might be passengers who were trying to escape. If they were, it was true that she'd hesitate to kill them. In the midst of these two opposing drives, Chané kept visualizing Huey's face and words.

However, at that point, Chané was seized by a nasty sensation. She felt an eerie presence, as though something ominous was looking her way, as though chills were enveloping her entire body.
Its source was behind the crawling figures.
A man in a white suit, dappled with red.
Instinctively, she knew this was the man who'd killed two of Goose's subordinates in the dining car.

⟺

"That doll's something else."

Ladd stood on the tail end of the dining car, gazing at the woman who was standing on the next car.

To think that chasing those crawling worms had led him to this hot little number!

Ladd was grateful to his own good instincts. He was really glad he'd gone after the crawling figures.

He caught occasional glimpses of the woman's eyes through the smoke. The intensity in those eyes! It wasn't a turn-off. For Ladd, the gaze held a terror that was actually pleasant. Here was a woman who was really worth killing. He wanted to dye those eyes with fear and despair this very minute.

Ladd, the boss of the white suits, was what you'd call an average human being. His uncle Placido's name was linked with a corner of underworld society, but he and his family had enjoyed an environment in which they could have been called quite ordinary people. There was no discernible cause for the darkness in his heart. You could say he'd been raised in what was, for Chicago, a completely normal family.

The impulse toward slaughter that dwelled in him wasn't the result of some sort of special experience. It had just popped into his head: human life and death, and the difference between people who died and people who didn't. He'd only thought it, plain and simple, as casually as if he was thinking up a dinner menu.

While his heart had been searching for a final answer, the process had gnawed away at his spirit. Before he knew it, his heart had sickened to the point where it was untreatable. Warped convictions had developed hardily, without him knowing how to compromise or accept them.

There had been no trauma, no pain, no particularly warped past. With no connection to any of these things, he'd degenerated into a completely twisted homicidal maniac. If there was one thing about him that was unusual, it was his speed of comprehension. It made his experience in killing people grow as quickly as if it were a part of him.

He did have his own convictions, after a fashion, but they were nothing more than an excuse known as "aesthetics." He wandered through the abnormal situation on this train as his desires led him.

And now, he'd discovered a supremely interesting toy.

A crosswind blew, revealing her whole body.

Taking that as a sign, Ladd yelled involuntarily:

"Heeeeeeey, ain'tcha cold out here in that dress——?"

⟺

Claire was perplexed.

He'd managed to send the signal from the conductors' room to the locomotive without incident; that was fine. A weird gunman had been there, and that had made it hard to get into the conductors' room, but a young tattooed guy and a big man had taken him away, so he'd managed to send the signal on schedule. In doing so, he'd bought himself a bit more time.

What had given him trouble had come after that.

Claire had gone under the train and made his way to the second-class carriages; nothing wrong there. He'd had no particular difficulty clinging to the protrusions on the side of the train and peeking in the window, either. The problem was that there were third-class passengers in the room where the white suits should have been. Two of them, at that.

One was a man who was enveloped in gray cloth from head to toe. He was a doctor named Fred, if memory served him right. As for the other... His face was smeared with blood, and Claire couldn't tell who he was. Claire thought he was a third-class passenger because his clothes were clearly the sort a back-alley delinquent would wear. But he wasn't discriminating on the basis of apparel: The only passengers who had been dressed like that today had been riding in the third-class car.

Apparently, the doctor who looked like a magician—Fred—was attempting to treat the bloodied man.

The act itself was only natural, but why was he doing it in a second-class compartment, and in the white suits' room, at that?

Question marks crossed Claire's mind.

Just then, the door to the room opened, and a man and woman in white came in. Claire recognized the pair: They were two of the three white suits who had been in the room where Czes was shot.

"......Oh."

On opening the door, Lua spoke in a voice no one else could hear.

"Who're you, dirtbags?!" her white-suited companion yelled after that.

They'd made it back to their own room, but why was the magician they'd met that evening there, and why was he treating the man Ladd had bloodied up a minute ago?

"Ah, is this your room?"

The gray magician spoke quietly.

"Your friend Ladd made me a kind offer, and I've taken him up on it. Thank you."

As he spoke, the magician resumed treating the bloody man.

The two white suits looked at one another. Their faces seemed to say, *What's going on? Imagine Ladd doing something like that...*

Without stopping his treatment, the magician nodded to the two white suits, politely:

"I'm terribly sorry to ask, but do you think you could help me move this patient to the bed?"

What's going on? From that exchange, it's hard to tell whether this Fred guy is friend or foe.

As Claire brooded outside the window, he abruptly realized that the woman in white was turned toward him.

He looked her way, too, and their eyes met. Claire thought the woman might scream, but she gazed at him quietly, without reacting at all.

Weird lady... Well, that's fine. I'll save this place for later.

On that thought, Claire slowly moved away from the window.

Just then.

He heard the noise of someone running over the roof at a ferocious pace. *Two* someones, actually, one after the other.

Instead of going down, Claire poked his upper body up over the edge of the roof. When he looked in the direction in which the footsteps had receded, two figures seemed to be making for the rear cars. From the colors, which were dimly illuminated by the moonlight, a woman in a black dress seemed to be chasing a man in white.

Descending again, Claire went under the train car. Unlike the ride-stealing woman, who'd moved like a monkey, his motions were both steady and fast. As his body squirmed mechanically, he looked like a huge crimson spider.

When he reached a connecting platform near the third-class car, Claire climbed up for a moment. He'd wanted to confirm the positions of that black suit and white suit, but it looked as though they might still be up on the roof.

Thinking he'd check the corridor, he peeked in through the window in the door—and frowned.

He could see a shadow walking stealthily down the third-class corridor. The figure was short, and Claire knew who it was right away, but a slight doubt appeared in his mind:

Didn't that boy die a few minutes back?

⟺

Czes went into one of the third-class compartments and sat down on an uncushioned bench. Beds were provided starting in second class. In third class, you slept in the seats.

The other rooms between the freight room and this place had had third-class passengers tied up in them. He'd checked room after room, quietly peeking in through the doors, until he'd finally reached an unoccupied compartment.

Even so, he hadn't seen any black suits. He'd assumed they'd be guarding the passengers they'd tied up. Although Czes wondered about this, he satisfied himself with the idea that the white suits had probably disposed of them.

For now, I'll monitor the situation from this room. It will be easier to work if I make my move after either the black suits or the white suits have eliminated the other group.

Czes quietly closed his eyes, deciding to rest for a little while. That said, to make absolutely sure he didn't really fall asleep, he was careful to keep his consciousness from drifting.

Just then, he heard the sound of the door opening slightly.

"!"

Immediately, Czes bolted upright, focusing all his nerves on the entrance to the room.

The crack in the door grew wider and wider, and what appeared, blocking the light from the corridor, was—a bizarre individual dressed in red, with blood on his face.

The figure in red bewildered Czes for a moment, but the second he noticed that a little of the cloth wasn't crimson, he realized what the color actually was. It wasn't the suit's original color. The cloth had been dyed by a massive amount of blood.

Because the other color that was still visible in places was white, Czes mistakenly assumed the man was one of the white suits.

"Who are you? One of Mr. Ladd's friends?"

He spoke in a child's voice, but the man didn't respond.

"What is it…? Who're you?"

A slight unease was beginning to grow inside him.

Ignoring Czes's words, the red man shut the door behind him. Now Czes was all alone with a strange man, and his anxiety increased.

This guy might be the immortal. Czes hadn't seen him in the dining car, but from the demeanor he wore, it wasn't impossible.

"Come on, say something. I'm Thomas, okay? I think you maybe have the wrong person."

He managed to give a false name easily. In other words, this mystery man wasn't an immortal. Inwardly, Czes heaved a great sigh of relief. As long as the other man wasn't deathless, there was nothing to fear.

However, at the phantom's first words, a wave of unease assailed his heart again.

"Why are you lying, Czes? Or rather, Czeslaw Meyer."

"H-how do you know my name?"

The red man didn't answer that question. Czes kept desperately searching the thread of his memories, thinking he must have met him somewhere. He felt as though he'd heard his voice before, but he couldn't remember whose it had been. He thought he might simply have a voice that resembled someone else's.

Czes never did realize that the man was the conductor who'd been checking the passenger list before boarding.

What is he? What the devil is this man? What are those eyes? The look in them is several times more terrifying than that Ladd fellow's. What is this? It's almost as if he isn't human. But that can't be. Unless… Wait. If the demon who created our immortality exists, then perhaps—

The wild tale he'd heard in the dining car surfaced in the boy's mind, and in spite of himself, he spoke the name aloud:

"Ra…Rail Tracer…?"

At the boy's murmur, the monster looked mildly mystified, and simultaneously rather pleased.

"Huh. You knew. I'm impressed."

The content of the tale Isaac had told replayed in Czes's mind. *If you do something bad, you'll get eaten by the Rail Tracer…*

The boy's pulse raced. The phantom took a step toward him.

"I am—the Rail Tracer."

With great self-confidence, Claire declared something that would have been nothing more than a tasteless joke to a normal listener.

However, Czes had seen his eyes, and he knew it wasn't a joke. In sharp contrast to the way he spoke, the man's eyes were filled with a dark light that seemed to be on the verge of devouring everything about his opponent.

"I know you're not a kid, and I know what you want… So I guess I'll go ahead and kill you."

Since the other guy wasn't a child, Claire didn't intend to show him any mercy. Czes was an enemy of the train, and he was also cooperating with the Runorata Family. If he was an enemy in two different ways, that was more than enough reason to eliminate him.

"Wah—waaaaaugh!"

Finding himself faced with a man who'd introduced himself as a legendary monster possibly capable of devouring him, Czes frantically rolled one sleeve up high. There was a leather band strapped around his arm, securing a sticklike object wrapped in cloth.

Czes hastily took the object from his arm and roughly tore off its wrapping.

What appeared from beneath the cloth was a sharp blade. It was a weapon very similar to a surgical scalpel but nearly twice as long.

Czes dropped into a crouch, then rushed the man.

Right in front of the phantom, he straightened, stretching up, and tried to slash his throat with the long scalpel. A silver streak drew a clean arc, heading for the man's throat.

Smack.

The man didn't move a single step. In a motion as if he were catching a mosquito, he grabbed Czes's arm easily, stopping it.

Then, before Czes could struggle, he'd completed his counterattack.

The phantom immobilized the blade with his right hand. At almost the same time, his left hand caught Czes's neck in an iron grip, then *tore off* a chunk of the flesh of his throat.

"Ah..."

A small cry escaped Czes. The phantom's left hand was dyed red, and blood dripped onto the floor. He took Czes's long scalpel, then kicked the little body away from him, hard.

Staggering violently, the boy retreated, then sank to the floor at the very back of the room, under the window.

The area around his carotid artery had been gouged out. In ordinary terms, no matter what happened, it wasn't a wound he could survive.

It's over.

Claire gazed at the fallen boy, then started to leave the room. However, feeling a strange sensation on his hand, he stopped. When he looked, wondering what was going on, the blood that coated that hand was trembling. The trembling definitely wasn't coming from his hand. The liquid itself was shivering.

What's this?

Czes's blood was falling from his right hand and down to the floor at a terrific pace. Not even a single drop of the boy's blood remained on Claire's hand.

The blood that had dripped onto the floor squirmed as if it was alive, creeping back to where it belonged—to Czes's body.

The blood that had splattered across the room merged with itself again and again, crawling up to Czes's wound.

"*Oh.* Never mind, then."

The moment the wound closed completely, Czes murmured cheerfully, speaking like a child.

"So that's all you've got. That wasn't worth getting startled over. I thought you might swallow me whole or something."

Getting to his feet as though nothing had happened, Czes spoke, giggling:

"Surprised? I'm immortal, you see."

Before his eyes, the phantom stopped moving. *That was easy,* Czes thought. At first he'd thought he was a monster, but apparently, he killed the same way humans did. That meant there was nothing to fear.

Of course: I'll use this guy. If I tell him I'll give him an eternal body, he may massacre the passengers in the dining car for me willingly.

Czes smiled brightly, deciding to ask his "favor" of the red man in front of him.

"Listen, could I ask you a—?"

"No."

Huh?

Czes's thoughts stalled for a moment. He hadn't even told him what the favor was yet.

"You're going to tell me to kill the people in the dining car, right? I'm not taking an order like that."

For the third time, unease welled up in Czes's heart.

How does he know that?

Czes's relaxed smile had disappeared. In exchange, the phantom's mouth warped as if he was truly entertained.

"Immortal, huh? Interesting."

Claire's hand flickered, and there was a small *thunk.*

It was the sound of the long scalpel sinking into Czes's forehead, right between his eyes.

Ferocious pain streaked through his head, but he managed to stay conscious, although his vision blurred and pain raced like lightning around his skull. Making practiced use of hands that wouldn't move well, he managed to pull the scalpel out.

The pain stopped, and his senses began returning to normal.

"That hurt quite a bit, but it isn't enough to kill me. Nothing is, really."

There was no point in pretending to be a child anymore. Czes changed his tone to that of an adult and started to search for ways to counter the monster in front of him.

For the moment, he'd managed to retake his weapon, but overpowering this man would be virtually impossible.

Besides, Czes had never dreamed he'd see his immortal body and let it go with nothing more than the comment "Interesting."

The scarlet phantom took a few steps toward Czes and spoke, popping his neck as he did so.

"All right. What should I do with you? If you're immortal, does that mean you'll be fine if I skin you or gouge out your eyes or crush your heart while you're still alive?"

Claire spoke indifferently, and Czes answered him with equal indifference:

"Go ahead. I'm more than used to that sort of pain."

"Yeah?"

Czes was remembering the various kinds of torment *he* had had inflicted on him. He'd experienced far too much of that sort of agony the phantom had described, back in the early days.

Glaring steadily at Claire, Czes began to speak in a quiet, intense voice:

"Have you ever had hot pokers stabbed into your eyes and ears? Has anyone made you soak in an acid bath? Have you been thrown into a fireplace alive? Someone I trusted tortured me like that every day. Do you know how that feels? I won't yield to brute violence like yours. My readiness for pain is in a completely different league!"

Having listened in silence, Claire took another step toward Czes and said:

"Is that it? That's seriously all you've got?"

"Wha…what?"

"That's no good. That's all hobbyist stuff. Hopelessly twisted hobbies. Well, I really can't understand interests like that, but—"

Another step, and he smacked Czes's cheek lightly with his hand.

"Have you ever had the meat *carefully* stripped off your arm while you're alive? Has anyone carved things into your arm bones afterward? Are you familiar with Chinese execution methods? With Japanese torture? Do you know what perverted European nobles did to prolong their lives?"

Claire stopped smacking Czes's cheek, and a monstrous color surfaced in his eyes. It was almost as if he was trying to absorb Czes's soul.

"Thanks to my job, I know tons of ways to inflict pain. Some of 'em are meant to be fatal, too."

At the sight of those eyes, Czes gave an inarticulate scream. Then he swung the scalpel in his hand with all his might…or tried to.

Click.

The next instant, Claire had trapped the long scalpel between his teeth. He'd caught Czes's hand along with it, and he bit the thin fingers clean off.

"Gyaah…aaah!"

Czes gave a dull scream, and blood gushed from his right hand.

Claire spit the scalpel and the clump of bloody flesh onto the floor, then restrained Czes's head with both hands and spoke, gently and quietly.

"Listen up, Czeslaw Meyer. You do seem to be prepared for pain to some extent. When you saw me, though, when you found yourself confronted with the Rail Tracer, what was that worry I saw in your eyes?"

He looked steadily into Czes's eyes. It was as though the nerves in Czes's face had locked up: He couldn't move, couldn't close his eyes or look away. Claire's eyes were that intense.

My body is beginning to shake, little by little, starting from my toes.

What is this? Am I...terrified? Of this monster in front of me—of the Rail Tracer, a monster from an absurd little fairy tale?!

"What scares you is the unknown. You think, somewhere, there may be pain and suffering the likes of which you've never experienced. It makes you far more afraid of the unknown than other people. Am I right? Because you think you know a little about pain, your fear of it is twice as great as anyone else's. Right?"

Czes's face was reflected in those monstrous eyes, and he saw his own consumed by terror. Child or adult, it didn't matter—the self that pretended to be a child, or the one that posed as an adult—because sometimes, Czes wasn't sure which of them was the real one. In that sense, this frightened face he saw was probably his true self.

Trapped by fear, Czes began to cry, without even being aware of it.

"I'll give it to you. I'll show you that unknown pain."

Wiping those tears away with his hand, Claire spoke to the boy, softly.

"Until you forget how to come back."

⟺

Rachel was under the train, holding her breath.

She'd found a gap that was just the right size for a person to lie down in, and she was reclining in that space, resting her arms and legs. She looked around, moving only her head, but she didn't see the red monster.

She'd been resting her limbs there for a little while now, but she couldn't seem to shake her unease about the monster. Trembling hard, she'd settled in for the time being, slowly regaining her composure.

Moments passed, and her mind grew steadily calmer.

Okay. Let's say I was seeing things.

She was actually well aware that that had been real, but she forced herself to think otherwise. In any case, the important thing now was what had happened in the dining car after that.

Just when she'd decided to go back to the dining car and see what things were like in there…

Krisssh.

In the spaces between the earsplitting roar of the moving train, she thought she heard a sound like breaking glass.

A breath later, something wrapped itself around the iron bar right next to her.

It was a familiar sight.

A bright red figure was jutting out horizontally, supported only by its legs, which it had hooked onto the underside of the train, and it had someone else in a body lock.

Then it pressed that someone's right hand against ground that raced past at ferocious speed—

Rachel thought she was going to be sick, but even then, she couldn't avert her eyes. It felt as if, the moment she looked away, that red monster would turn toward her. There was another reason for her nausea: The person the monster was killing was a boy who was still quite young. She recognized him. It was the kid who'd been talking with the weird gunman and his friends in the dining car.

The boy's thin right arm and both his legs were gone. He had to have died ages ago, so why do all this?

As she trembled, with that question circling through her mind, a metal piece on the cuff of her coveralls came into contact with the iron around her and began making a small noise.

That tiny, chattering *click* should have been drowned out by the roar of the train. Even Rachel didn't hear the metallic sound.

But the crimson catastrophe caught it clearly.

Its head swiveled her way. The reflected light from the ground was behind it, and she couldn't clearly make out its expression. And yet the monster most certainly turned toward Rachel and murmured:

"Ride-stealing girl…"

"NOOOOOOOOOOOOOO!"

Screaming at the top of her lungs, Rachel fled toward the front of the train. As she went, she hung so insecurely that her back nearly brushed the ground, but she could move much faster this way. Clinging to the train like a sloth, yet moving a hundred times faster, Rachel vanished into the darkness.

While Claire had been inflicting various kinds of pain on Czes, the kid hadn't been able to take it anymore and had attempted to jump out the window.

He'd broken the glass in the big window and tried to escape, but Claire had caught him in his arms right before he managed it and had almost fallen down the side of the train. At the very last second, on the spur of the moment, he'd caught the piping between the train's wheels with his legs and had managed to keep from falling off entirely.

At that point, Claire had wondered what would happen if he dropped bits of Czes off the train (Would they chase after the kid?) and had begun pressing Czes's arms and legs to the ground.

When only Czes's left arm remained, Claire's sharp ears picked up an irregularity.

He twisted his head and upper body toward the noise, and there was the train jumper from a little while back.

The moment Claire spoke to her, she gave a scream that pierced through the sound of the train. Before he could stop her, she fled at a speed that impressed even him.

At that point, Claire froze abruptly. Holding Czes's body in his right arm, he took the rope from his coat with his left—the thin rope he'd picked up in the freight room. The orchestra had probably used it to bind up their cargo.

Claire dexterously used it to tie Czes into the space between the wheels, then left him and started off, under the train.

Not good, not good. Never mind this guy, I have to get rid of the black suits and white suits. I owe that ride-stealing girl for yanking

*me back to reality. As thanks, I guess I'll just turn her over to the cops
and let that be the end of it.*

As Claire was leaving, he spoke a couple of words to Czes, although
he didn't know whether he was conscious.

"We'll save the rest for later. I'm going to keep this up until you
go insane."

Czes's hazy mind heard faint voices speaking, directly above him.
"What is it?"

"...C'mere a second. Look at this."

Just after Claire had gone, two black suits poked their heads out of
the third-class compartment.

⟺

A group of five black suits had split into two smaller groups in front
of the third-class car. The group of three had reached the freight car.

What they saw there was a corpse without a lower half, lying in a
lake of blood.

"'S awful..."

They'd been terrified by the sight of their comrade's corpse lying
in the first freight room, but they'd managed to regain their composure. The wireless set was still beside him, so they hastily contacted
Goose.

"—That's the situation, and the wireless wasn't damaged, so we—
Yes, yes, that's right, there's just one body. We're about to leave for
the conductors' room— What? —Yes. Yes.

"—Understood. All right."

Switching off the wireless, the man who'd made contact turned to
face the other two.

Then, keeping an eye on his surroundings, he carefully informed
his comrades of the order.

"Code Beta has been invoked... On the condition that there's an
opportunity while she's fighting the white suit, anyway."

On hearing that, the tension in the pair's expressions grew.

"They're really doing it? Miss Chané…"

"Don't discuss the content of the operation."

The man who was acting as leader examined their surroundings even more carefully.

However, just when he'd confirmed that the room was completely empty of human shapes, a hyper voice came down to them from the ceiling.

"Say, about that. Think you could gimme some details?"

No sooner had it spoken than a white shadow dropped down from the ceiling and slashed the throat of the man who'd been next to the leader. The white shadow—Ladd—gripped the throwing knife Chané had thrown at him up on the roof in his right hand.

"Man, this is fun. Oh-man-oh-man-oh-man-oh-maaan, I tell ya, hanging from the steel beams up there ain't easy."

Without giving his opponents time to raise their guns, Ladd leaped at the enemy leader. In a heartbeat, he'd captured his back and was holding the knife against his neck.

"All right, all right, all right, drop your gun. And you, the sissy-looking fella over there, you drop yours, too. If you shoot, you're probably gonna plug this guy."

At Ladd's voice, the black-suit leader ground his teeth in frustration and dropped his gun. On the other hand, his timid-looking companion dropped his gun, turned tail, and ran out of the room.

"How 'bout that. He split. Damn, that was cold."

As Ladd watched the black suit's retreating back, entertained, he began talking to himself.

"Well, I'm not gonna call him a coward. Seeing me and running is the, whaddaya call it, the normal reaction. Besides, I just ran off a second ago myself and hid under the ceiling."

Cackling, he held the knife against the black suit's neck and forced him to move.

He closed the freight room door, then marched the black suit over to a corner.

"Man oh *man*, this is fun! I've never been the guy who ran before!

That doll is outta sight! You better compliment her, or actually, *I'll* compliment her! But I'm gonna kill her!"

The tip of the knife scraped against his neck in time with his laughter. The terrified black suit waited for the white suit's next words.

The white suit abruptly calmed down and began to sink the tip of his knife into the black suit's throat.

"You guys really are total amateurs. The only awesome thing about you is your weapons. At first I thought you were a bunch of army guys, and I was psyched, y'know? I thought I'd found me some military fellas who were completely off-guard for the first time ever. But one good look at you and my expectations were shot all to hell. Except for that dame, keh-keh."

Smirking, he sank the blade in another fraction of an inch.

"Chané is that broad's name, and the white suit she was fighting was me, yeah? C'mon, fill me in… She's on your team, right? Why're you guys gonna kill her?"

Little by little, the tip of the knife cut into the black suit's throat.

$$\Leftrightarrow$$

Under a first-class carriage, Rachel shivered, all alone.

Why is this happening? Why, why, why, why…? What was that monster? Do they have a monster working as the conductor on this train?

That monster's shaped like a human, but there's no way it's human on the inside! At first I thought it was only killing the black suits, but… To think it would butcher a little kid like that… That red monster really doesn't have a human heart.

How long had she been thinking the same thing and trembling? When the gun battle had broken out in the dining car, she'd barely even blinked, but now terror dominated her, body and soul.

As an info gofer, she'd waded into a variety of dangerous situations. She'd come very close to being killed several times. However, that had been nothing compared with the fear she felt now.

Mafia and flying bullets were terrors she could understand. They definitely existed, and she'd walked into those terrors completely prepared for them. Of course there had been a few times when the fear had been greater than what she'd prepared for, but it hadn't been anything she couldn't get through.

However, that crimson creature was in a whole different league. It was a being she couldn't understand. She couldn't even begin to imagine how to deal with it, or how she should prepare for it.

If there was one thing she did understand, it was that, as a ride-stealer, she absolutely must not let it catch her... Although she wouldn't have wanted that thing to catch her even if she *hadn't* been train jumping.

She had reached the locomotive. It would be dangerous to crawl through a space that was crowded with the boiler and other equipment. Having run out of places to go, Rachel had maneuvered until she was horizontal and then had lain down on the metal fittings beside the coupling. That said, since there wasn't much space under the train, horizontal was about the only position she could take.

In the darkness, the gravel that was spread under the tracks reflected the moonlight. That light was the only way to combat the darkness. Of course, it was very nearly useless, but still.

I'll never get anywhere if I just sit here. For now, Rachel decided to see how things looked in the first-class carriages. Compared with that scarlet nightmare, she much preferred dealing with black suits and machine guns.

Rather than wait where she was, she'd chosen to move around on her own and run until she was safe. She had no intention of being caught up in any sort of trouble. As long as she could get clean away, that was enough for her.

Carefully poking her head out from between the cars, she looked at the side of the first-class carriage.

Just as on the other cars, the decorative designs on the side could be used as handholds.

She grabbed one of the pieces, flattening herself against the side of the car as though she were rock climbing. Anyone who was not very used to this would probably have fallen off the train and into the afterlife during the maneuver.

Ever since she was a child, Rachel had run simulations that assumed all sorts of circumstances on stopped trains. Compared with going up the perfectly flat side of a normal train, climbing this gaudy, heavily ornamented carriage was easy.

She wondered if it would be better to climb up on top of the locomotive; she might not be found there. The thick smoke would hide her, and there probably wasn't anyone who would go all the way out there.

She entertained that idea for a moment, but aside from the fact that the smoke might suffocate her, she had no idea what the temperature in the area around the smokestack might be; that was uncharted territory for her. Deciding to think about it after she'd climbed up to the roof, she quietly approached the window. For now, she thought, she'd see what things were like inside, but—

Rachel stealthily peeked in, then regretted it.

I wish I hadn't seen that.

What she'd seen was a young girl and her mother with their arms and legs bound with ropes. There was one black suit with a machine gun beside them.

No, no, no, no! Don't get involved! If you get involved, you'll die! You walk into danger for information, but you can't risk your life for something that won't bring in any money!

Desperately lecturing herself, she kept climbing toward the roof.

Her father's figure rose in her mind. Her father, who'd been cut off by his company and had died burdened only with hardship. The man the company had abandoned to save its own skin.

Hold it, you! That and this are completely different things! Listen, your life is already on the line here! If you waste it because of cheap reasoning like that, you're denying your whole life up to this point!

She scolded herself frantically, but it was too late. Her father's face clung to her mind, and it wouldn't let go.

What are you doing?! I said no! You steal rides all the time; doing something like this now won't make up for any of that! So stop already! You have to stop! Don't let yourself—

Before she knew it, her body was right above the window, and she'd lowered one leg a little—

No, no, no! You've got to stop! You have to stop! Stop—

Then her toe lightly kicked the window a few times.

…Too late now.

The window opened, and the man in black poked his head out.

When she saw him at the lower edge of her field of vision, she made up her mind.

Since it's too late now, I'll go all the way.

She let go of the wall with both hands and fell, letting gravity take over. She felt the soles of her boots come down on something soft, and for a moment, she stopped falling. The instant she felt that, she got an underhanded grip on the windowsill with her fingers…and threw all her weight onto the man's upper body.

The goon lost his balance and began to fall, bending over backward. Rachel promptly moved her feet forward, as if she were walking on the black suit's stomach, and got her legs into the train. As if in exchange, the man fell outside. Watching him roll away, she thought, *I don't want to be a murderer, so please don't die.* That was how Rachel touched down into the room.

⇔

When Claire reached the dining car, he peeked in from outside to see how things looked.

There were two guards within, holding machine guns.

"No help for it."

Murmuring quietly, Claire closed one eye and went down under the car. Then he reached out for a box with a yellow mark on it, located in the very middle of the car's underside.

Several small levers protruded from the box. He set a hand on one of them.

"If they're going to spend money on stuff like this, I wish they'd put in a wireless system between the conductors' room and the engine room. And anyway, putting the generator exchange switch under the car... That's a design flaw no matter how you look at it."

This was the key part of one of the *Flying Pussyfoot*'s distinguishing features: a system that generated power for the electric lights from the wheels of each carriage.

Once, a turbine behind the safety valve of the locomotive's boiler had taken care of everything, including lighting the passenger cars. In time, the electricity from that turbine had been switched to exclusively power the lamps in and around the locomotive, and so it no longer went to the passenger cars.

On this train, electricity was generated from the wheel axles, and the electric wiring for each car was independent. As a result, the system—which was unique to this train—generated more electricity than normal, and it was possible to make the train's interior as bright as day.

One of the switchboards was under the car, and Claire had reached for that switchboard's selecting switch.

"If someone sneaked under the train, it would be easy for them to cause a power outage...like this."

He pulled the lever and, in almost the same moment, quickly exited the car.

"All right, I guess I'll go push myself a bit."

Muttering this, he began doing acrobatics on the side of the moving train.

Inside the dining car, which had gone dark, a scream went up. At the same time, working from the outside, he flung open a window at the rear of the car.

"What's that?!"

One of the black suits came over, holding a gun. Claire withdrew his arms and waited for the man to thrust the gun outside.

Immediately, the gun muzzle was shoved through the window. Apparently, they weren't used to unexpected situations. What a bunch of morons.

As he thought this, Claire promptly grabbed the gun and dragged it toward himself.

"Whoa..."

He pulled the black suit's body over, then corrected his grip, grabbing the man's arm. Destabilizing his balance with just one hand, Claire yanked him down with tremendous force.

He threw the man from the train. It wasn't certain he'd die, but Claire didn't have time to finish him off before dropping him.

Then he *ran along* the ornamentation on the train's side.

The sculptured reliefs created slight projections, and he ran on top of them, leaning forward, making for the front of the train.

Whenever it seemed as though he might drift away from the side, he stretched out his left hand, grabbed a window frame, and pulled himself back upright by force.

Run, run, run. By forcing a vision to come true, Claire made that nightmare a part of reality. The one destined to see the nightmare was the other black suit.

A man running soundlessly on the side of the train. Seen from a distance, it would probably have looked as though he were running on thin air beside the train.

In the darkness, the passengers saw a red shadow running outside, illuminated by moonlight. When they did, the screams in the car increased explosively.

By the time the black suit, between two tables, opened the window beside him, it was too late.

Claire was already there, and before the man could train his gun on him, Claire had grabbed his arm.

"Applause, please: I've never done this before, and I did it on the first try... I worked really hard. All right?"

He hauled the black suit toward him, whispering quietly in his ear. Then, as the man shuddered with terror, he threw him out of the train without the slightest hesitation.

Claire went under the car again, quickly returned to the switch-board, and threw the lever.

When he went back to the window and looked in, different black suits were there.

"They just keep popping up like cockroaches..."

Sounding half-disgusted, he got rid of one on the coupling. The other seemed to have seen him, and he ran off toward the first-class compartments.

I guess that's not a problem. As long as they're focused on me, they probably won't hurt the passengers.

Giving a small nod, he started back toward the rear cars.

It was almost time to send the signal to the locomotive.

$$\Longleftrightarrow$$

Where is that man?

Up on the roof, just over the conductors' room, Chané was focusing every nerve she had.

Having lost sight of Ladd in the neighborhood of the freight room, she'd returned to the roof and was surveying the area.

That man is dangerous. I have to get rid of him immediately. If I don't, he'll be my greatest obstacle. He may also prove to be a difficult roadblock for Huey.

Although she had no grounds for it, she felt something decidedly close to certainty, and so she sought out the red-dappled white suit. Having determined that she wouldn't find him by moving around at random, she'd decided to look out over the entire train again from the roof, but—

Her target appeared on his own.

Quite naturally, wearing the sort of expression he would have worn to meet a friend.

"Hey."

At the sight of Ladd's face, with its suspiciously broad smirk, Chané felt even more certain: She really did have to dispose of this man.

Although she didn't know her opponent's true identity, thoughts that could have been taken as paranoid delusions continued to grow inside her... Though they weren't entirely delusions.

"How've you been, my kitten? Were you lonely without me?"

Ladd gave an unpleasant smile. In response, Chané wordlessly drew her knife.

Her opponent didn't seem to have his rifle. On confirming this, she lowered her stance, preparing to break into a run.

"That's cold, Chané."

Chané stopped moving.

How does this man know my name?

Upon seeing her confusion, Ladd nodded, satisfied.

"I know everything about you, see. Like how the rest of 'em hate you, and how you hate 'em right back, and how you're Master Huey Laforet or whoever's favorite, and how you're a fanatical believer in this Huey guy, too."

He glibly trotted out meaningless information. As if to say she didn't want to hear any more of it, Chané dropped into a crouch again.

"And how your Master Huey fella is immortal."

Once again, Chané stopped in her tracks. The situation seemed to entertain this Ladd. He knew everything, and on top of that, he'd hit his opponent with critical comments whenever she started to move.

Chané decided not to listen to what the man said anymore. Lowering her stance for the third time, she launched herself at her foe. No matter what the man knew, she absolutely had to kill him now. Her stance was frighteningly low; she intended to slash at Ladd's legs with her knife.

However—and there was no telling what he was thinking—Ladd made his own stance about as low as Chané's and began charging at *her*.

Not only that, but he kept right on bantering as he did it.

"But hey, listen, I'm a bit bummed out."

Ladd's actions weren't what Chané had expected, and she hesitated for a moment. As a result, there was a very slight delay before she thrust her knife out.

"See, you…"

Ladd's voice receded. To Chané, it looked as though he'd been abruptly blown away.

At the same time, a fierce shock ran through her jaw.

Ladd had actually stepped within range of her knife strikes, then launched himself into a somersault. He'd done a backflip from his low stance, and in the process, he'd slammed his toes into Chané's jaw.

Her body had been as low as it would go, but now it was knocked upward all in a rush, and she rolled over and over toward the back of the car. She made the last revolution intentionally, in order to get back into her stance.

"See, I thought you were, y'know, crazier, like you'd been possessed by a Martian or something, but you're just some fanatic, in love with love? What're you, a kid in her teens? Ah, yeah, I guess you're actually out of your teens, huh? Say, don't you think that Huey fella's just taking you for a ride? Hmm?"

Those words flipped Chané's switch completely. She'd never thought of Huey as a lover. If she'd been able to do so, it might have been for the best, but she was Huey's daughter. In her heart, that was something forbidden, and in fact, she'd always adored him as a father. However, to others, they looked like a man and woman who were about the same age. Someone who actually had a daughter would probably have been able to tell that their relationship wasn't a romantic one, but unfortunately, the black suit who'd told Ladd about Chané hadn't even had a girlfriend.

Chané's eyes opened wide, and she lowered her stance even more than before. Then she ran at Ladd with the launch velocity of a bullet.

"Hya-ha-ha-ha, are ya mad? Are ya mad?"

When he saw Chané's expression, Ladd also realized that the situation might not be that simple. However, he had absolutely no intention of correcting himself. On the contrary: If his opponent was angry, her actions would be easier to predict, and that was all to the good.

Cackling, Ladd stood his ground. However, it didn't unsettle Chané this time. She got ready to slash Ladd's throat along the trajectory she'd first visualized. When her body was right in front of him, she shot up to a higher stance.

Mimicking the path of an airplane in steep ascent, Chané's knife sliced through the wind.

Having anticipated this, Ladd swayed with abnormal agility, dodging the strike. At the same time, he bent his knees deeply, lowering himself. Then he tried to sink a fist into her defenseless body.

However, sensing that Chané's form had bent drastically, he immediately scooted to the side.

Chané's legs swung up with terrific force. She'd attempted to unleash a somersault kick, just as Ladd had done a moment ago.

"No ya don't."

Ladd promptly grasped the situation, and while Chané was still airborne, he kicked her to the side, hard.

Once again, she rolled fast, over and over, and dropped off the side of the train.

"Huh? Done already? Already? That's boring, ain't it? Ain't that sad?"

Just then, a satisfying sound rang out: *kashunk.*

"What the...?"

Ladd looked down over the side and saw something unbelievable.

Chané had stabbed the knives she held in each hand into the wall, keeping herself on the side of the train. She pulled out the knives and stabbed them back in again by turns, beginning to climb the wall at tremendous speed.

Kashunk kashunk kashunk kshunk kshunk shunk shunk

Gradually increasing the speed at which the knives stabbed and left the train, she climbed back up so fast she seemed to be running straight up the wall.

"Whoa!"

Just as Ladd dodged, Chané flew up from the side of the train like a rocket, passing right by him.

He thought he'd evaded her by a hair, but a cut opened in his right ear, and a little blood trickled out.

"Sorry 'bout that: You may actually be a Martian. Bet you really have about eight legs, don'tcha?"

Having broken out in a cold sweat for the first time, Ladd quietly clenched his fists and began bouncing, light on his feet. Chané also shifted her grip on her knives, beginning to gauge the distance between herself and Ladd.

Then, in that moment, something odd happened.

The two of them were currently fighting on the last car, the one with the conductors' room and the spare freight room. The only thing in the conductors' room should have been the two corpses. And yet—

The lamps on either side of the car lit up brightly, several times.

They were the lights that signaled that nothing was wrong with the train, but...who in the world was flashing them?

The flashing stopped, and the pair faced each other in silence.

Nothing was going to happen. Having come to that conclusion, Ladd began spitting out words once more, trying to make his opponent lose her cool.

"Say, Chané, did you know your black-suited pals are gunning for you? From what I hear, they're gonna take advantage of this confusion and rub you out."

Chané didn't seem the least bit upset by those words. She'd already been aware of that, and she'd been thinking about getting rid of Goose and the others as well.

"They say you were actually against this operation, yeah? It sounds like you weren't happy about taking hostages and killing brats. Kind of a cream puff, ain'tcha? I guess that Huey fella didn't like that stuff to begin with, but you'll never get anywhere like that, y'know? I can see why the black suits would want to sell you down the river."

Still silent, Chané listened to Ladd's words. Possibly because the events of a moment before had been rough on her, she seemed to be desperately holding her feelings in check, keeping herself from getting worked up.

"You're fighting a revolution, you're starting a gunfight with the Man, but you don't want to do anything that ain't fair, and you don't want to kill normal folks? Nice dream, sweetheart, but you better wake the hell up. What, is that Huey rube so tough he can afford to think about other folks' lives while he's fighting a war? If so, then it kinda makes sense, but that's the type of guy I hate most! You can't pull that stunt unless you think you're absolutely safe! Dammit! That's just unforgivable!"

After getting himself worked up for a while, he gave a little smirk and lowered his voice:

"Want me to tell you what I'm gonna do after I get off this train, first thing?"

Warping his mouth hugely, ogling his opponent's body slowly and lewdly, he said:

"Kill Huey Laforet."

At that simple threat, Chané's heart instantly froze over.

"I thought it was weird, y'know? I always thought terrorists were the type who were A-okay with taking dirt naps, but your black-suited pals were all relaxed as hell, like they were thinking, 'I'm never gonna die.' Well, sure: Once this job is done, they might be getting immortal bodies."

He kept taking short, quick boxing steps, simultaneously raising the tension and volume of his voice.

"Lemme be honest here. I'm not all that into killing you. Your ideas are completely soft, but you seem like you're putting your life on the line. So I had this idea, see! I thought it'd be more fun to kill that absolute being of yours, Huey Laforet!"

Ladd abruptly stopped his footwork, turned to Chané, and yelled straight at her. As if he were truly happy. As if he were really enjoying himself. As if toying with Chané's heart gave him a rush.

"Anyway, I'm gonna kill 'im. Maybe he's immortal, but I'll kill 'im. If he doesn't die, I'll cut his head off his body and sink one of 'em at the North Pole and the other at the South Pole. Right in front of you. I'm gonna take that laid-back bastard who thinks he's safe because he can't die and give him a lesson in how tough life really is. I'll school him so hard he can't stand it. Course, even if he *says* he can't stand it, I ain't gonna stop. Well?! What are you gonna do, Chané?! Hya-ha-ha-ha-ha-ha-ha-ha!"

It was a truly stale line, but Ladd knew very well that this sort of woman latched onto clichéd challenges the best.

A great shudder ran through Chané, body and soul. If the earlier taunt had been an ignition switch, these words were a detonator. Focusing all her strength into the points of her knives, she tried to sprint straight at Ladd.

…But the knives wouldn't move.

The tips of the blades she held in either hand had been caught between somebody's fingers and immobilized. Until that very moment, she hadn't noticed.

A man in red was standing there, right in front of her… But that should have been impossible: Right up until a moment ago, when her vision had gone white with anger, she was sure there hadn't been anyone in front of her.

He'd sprung out of nowhere.

That was the perfect way to describe the situation.

The monster had finally shown itself to them.

The red demon—the Rail Tracer.

As he kept Chané's knives still, holding them between his thumbs and forefingers, the red shadow murmured quietly:

"Don't poke holes in the conductors' room. You grazed my ear."

At first, neither Ladd nor Chané understood what the man was saying. After giving it a little thought, they grasped the substance of what he'd said. Apparently, when Chané had used her knives to climb up the side of the train a moment ago, this man had been just on the other side of that wall.

"If you get it, then apologize."

At the red shadow's words, in spite of herself, Chané nodded. Forgetting even her recent anger at Ladd, she lowered both hands and bobbed her head in a bow. If the other black suits had been there, every one of them would have doubted their eyes. Ladd certainly did.

"At least give me an 'I'm sorry.'"

At that, Chané pointed at her throat, then shook her head. Apparently, for some reason, she couldn't speak.

"Ah. Sorry about that. My bad."

The red shadow apologized meekly, then began to stride over the roof, turning back to face them when he neared the coupling that was linked to the freight cars.

"Carry on."

And so…the bright red monster cut in on Ladd and Chané's fight.

"I'll kill whoever survives."

⇔

Lua wanted someone to kill her. She wanted it so badly that she'd even forgotten why she wanted to die. Feeling that suicide was idiotic, she'd searched for someone who would kill her. She wanted to find someone who would have fun as they killed her. In the end, she wanted to die making somebody happy.

Then she'd met Ladd. He might have more fun killing her than anyone else on the planet would.

"Once I kill off everyone in the world who wants to live more than you do, at the very end, I'll pull out all the stops, give it everything I've got, and kill you deader 'n dead. So don't die before then, and stick with me. Got it?"

That had been how he'd proposed. She knew it wasn't a trick to get her to live longer. It was something he actually thought, from the bottom of his heart.

She also believed that Ladd would make it happen. Ladd had never failed when he tried to kill somebody, and she couldn't even imagine somebody else killing him.

…Until she saw that red shadow.

When Lua had made eye contact with the red shadow that had looked in through the window of this room a moment ago, her heart had wavered dramatically. It wasn't out of any sort of terror or love. It was enormous anxiety. *He'll be killed—that monster with the dreadful eyes is going to kill Ladd. Ladd can't win against that!*

She'd realized what the horrible light that filled the monster's eyes really was.

The intent to kill. Those eyes had been made of pure murderous intent. Lua had noticed it right away. After all, it was something she was used to seeing: Those eyes were exactly like Ladd's when he was killing someone. If there was one difference, it was that the strength of the will in those eyes was beyond comparison with Ladd's.

She'd felt, very strongly, that it was clearly a being from another world, a world different from theirs. Its strength of will far surpassed humans'. Even more terrifying was the fact that, in the end, the monster had gone away without killing them. She didn't know the reason, but she understood that even with that immense murderous intent in its eyes, the monster had been in control of itself.

Ladd was invincible where humans were concerned, but against a monster, things would be different. He'd be killed, Ladd was going to be killed—

"Are you all right, young lady?"

A low voice brought her back to herself. She was in a second-class compartment, their group's room.

In front of her, the gray-robed magician had just finished treating the man.

"There's a lot of life in your eyes now. Unlike before."

"……Huh?"

Lua responded with a question in a scarcely audible voice. As she looked at the magician's face, she realized something.

This man is like me. He wants to die…

Possibly he'd understood the significance of the gaze Lua turned on him. The man spoke quietly.

"Right in the middle of the Great War, I joined up as a military doctor. I went to Verdun. So many of us died, enemies and allies alike. Once, when I looked around, for as far as I could see, I was the only living soul."

He spoke, not wallowing in painful memories, but simply and indifferently.

"I thought, 'Ah, is this punishment?' If I'd treated more people, would I have been spared that sight? Intriguingly, no matter what battlefield I went to after that, right to the end of the Great War, I didn't die. I hadn't been running around trying to escape, mind you. No matter how great my injuries were, my life was always spared."

To Lua, the man's story seemed like a tale from some distant world. The cloth over his face had slipped slightly, exposing the hideously burned flesh beneath. It was likely that his entire body was covered with scars like that one.

"If it was divine punishment, and I ran from it through suicide, I would probably be given a heavier punishment. That is why I treat people: I see it as my duty to save as many souls who want to live as possible. Until God allows me to die."

When he'd said that much, he looked at Lua's face.

"It looks as if you've found something you must do. Unlike earlier, your eyes are alive. I don't know whether it's from terror or anger or sadness. However…"

On hearing those words, Lua slowly stood up.

"Hey, Lua, where are you going?"

"Not far… I'll be right back, so wait for me…"

Saying this to her white-suited companion, Lua departed the room. Behind her, the gray man spoke to her, in a dull voice:

"Once you've done what you need to do, perhaps you could return to being dead… No, forget that. It felt as though someone with eyes like mine was disappearing, and it made me a little lonely for a moment, that's all…"

With the man's words at her back, Lua left to find Ladd. The doctor's sentiment hadn't been an encouraging one. His words had been spoken in a way that plunged her into greater unease. Yet what had made her so uneasy, when all the man had done was speak methodically about himself? It was almost as if the man…was Death.

When she'd thought Ladd was the strongest, her instincts had been correct. She would never doubt that. Only, precisely because that was true, she could trust this instinct as well. Ladd mustn't fight him, mustn't defy him, mustn't meet him. That red shadow was bound to bring Ladd misfortune.

Remembering the eyes of the red man from a moment before, Lua quietly ran through the train.

⟺

The sudden intruder left Ladd and Chané unable to move. The sky was still gloomy, and they couldn't really see the man's expression. They knew just one thing for certain: He wore clothes that were dyed red, from head to toe. Ladd was "dappled with red," but in this man's case, the simple term "bright red" was enough.

Ladd was the first to speak, breaking a long silence:

"Who're you?"

His tone held a clear wariness that was quite unlike him, and he began to turn very slightly away from Chané, toward the scarlet watcher.

"Don't worry about it."

The red man's answer was simple as well. However, Ladd was convinced of one thing:

This is probably the guy who offed Dune.

What had convinced him was the sight of the clothes he was wearing. Although they'd been dyed red with blood, the design was definitely the one that belonged to the train's conductors. In addition, in order to get splashed with this much of your victim's blood, you'd need to kill very messily. These two conditions overlapped, making Ladd certain that this was the culprit who'd killed his friend.

He didn't know who this conductor who'd killed Dune was, but it was clear at a glance that he wasn't anybody decent.

The not-at-all-decent man spoke words that were, as expected, a bit odd:

"Think of me as talking air."

"Oh yeah?"

Ladd gave that arrogant answer an insolent response. However, his intent to kill this man who'd slaughtered his friend was already at max.

He'd been planning to kill his friend's enemy, anyway. He took a bloodied throwing knife out of his coat and, with no hesitation, threw it at the crimson man. The silver rod, dulled with blood, headed straight for the man's throat.

"If you're air, don't *talk*!"

"That's harsh."

Neatly catching the thrown knife, the red-stained man—Claire—smiled quietly.

A moment's silence.

"Hold it. Didn't you just do something really unnatural?"

"Not at all. See? I caught the hilt, so my hand didn't get cut. That's natural, right?"

He chuckled, sending a response meant to taunt him back. That bumped Ladd's intent-to-kill gauge up past its maximum. He didn't care what the other guy did. *What I really can't stand are this monster's eyes. Those eyes are seriously bad news. A normal person probably wouldn't even be able to look at 'em straight on. But above and beyond that, I can't forgive him! What the hell is this guy, this bastard?! When he caught the doll's knives back there, and when I threw the knife at him, his eyes didn't even flicker. He's got the kinda smell I hate most. The same as some phony pacifist who spouts random crap when he only knows about war from the radio and the papers. The same as a mafia boss who makes his men do all the risky stuff and takes the biggest share of the money for himself, when he don't do squat. Like that guy from a while back, the one who looked like a kid... Nah, this fella's even worse!*

Ladd's eyes sprang wide open, fiercely, and he launched himself into a run, heading for Claire.

Leaning forward, he got in close and attempted to unleash a barrage of fists.

Just as he thought his first attack would hit home, Claire evaded it in a way that would normally have been impossible.

"Say what?"

Right before Ladd's eyes, Claire's body receded. He spread his arms wide, bending backward. Or, no, this went beyond simply bending: He just *fell* backward. Even though the roof of the train ran out right at his feet.

Ladd thought his opponent had thrown himself onto the tracks. Claire's body had nothing to support it, and naturally, it disappeared down below.

However, that thought only lasted a moment. Claire's upper body, which should have been gone, bounded back up from the side of the train.

Claire had hooked his legs from the knees down onto the roof of the train, flattening his upside-down body against the side. Then, using part of the ornamentation as a handhold, he'd launched his torso back up.

In a motion like a spring-action doll, Claire's upper body returned to the roof...where he promptly rammed his head into Ladd's chin.

In spite of himself, Ladd retreated a few steps but began to shift directly into a counterattack.

However, he caught a flash of silver out of the corner of his eye and hastily dropped into a crouch. Immediately afterward, the blade of a knife skimmed over his head, and a few hairs danced on the wind.

"*That does it*, you damn broad!"

Ladd dropped back a few steps, glaring at Chané, who'd paid out that knife attack. Chané wasn't looking at the red shadow anymore. She'd focused all her attention on killing Ladd.

However, Claire's voice broke that concentration easily. Although it was laid-back, the voice was too intimidating to ignore.

"You're Chané, right? Was the stuff that guy said a minute ago true?"

Without showing any particular emotion, Claire quietly asked Chané a question.

"Uh, you know: about how you were actually against this operation, and how you don't really want to kill people. How the Huey fella isn't into that sort of thing, either."

Chané wasn't sure whether she should answer the red shadow's abrupt inquiry. She could have ignored it, but it felt as though ignoring it would mean denying herself and Huey, so she nodded emphatically in response.

"I see. Well, good. In that case, do you want me to help you out a little?"

"Huh?"

At this sudden offer, Ladd gave an idiotic-sounding cry, and Chané looked startled.

"Wait a minute, hold the phone, you ruddy monster! That's a bit weird, ain't it?! I don't really get it, but you're the one who's been going around bumping off the black suits and my pals, yeah?!"

"Right. What's the problem?"

"What the hell?! Then why are you telling her you'll help her out all of a sudden?! You killed *my* pals!"

Claire answered Ladd's perfectly natural yell with zero hesitation:

"Huh? Well, from what you were saying a minute ago…it sounds like she's actually one of the good guys."

At that answer, as expected, even Ladd fell silent for a bit.

"I heard you screaming, see," Claire offered. "If she has to go along with this to save somebody who's important to her, well… You've obviously got more than a couple screws loose, and it's easier to sympathize with her, and besides, I feel kinda sorry for her."

At that point, finally, anger welled up inside Ladd.

"Quit jerking me around, monster. What's that? You're feeling a little sympathy for this broad? Who the hell are you? Just how soft in the *head* are you?! Hah! And here I was wondering what sort of big, scary monster you were! You're *nothing*! You're just some sick-making hypocrite! Are you one of those guys? If kids with guns came at you on a battlefield, would you feel bad for them and save them, instead of killing the buggers? That's exactly what you're saying, low-watt!"

His scream was technically a sound argument, but Claire didn't even blink.

"Yeah, I'd save them. What about it?"

"Huh?"

"Well, it would also depend on whether the kids ticked me off or not, but still."

With an expression that seemed to say, *Why would you ask me something so obvious?* Claire proceeded to relate an idea that would normally be unthinkable to Ladd in a matter-of-fact voice.

"I think 'feeling bad for people' is one of those things you càn do because you've got the leeway to do it. I'm good there. I mean, say that Chané girl took a slash at me from behind: I could block it without breaking a sweat. If those kids cut loose with their machine guns while I was feeling sorry for them, I could dodge, no problem. Sure, they might get mad and tell me not to feel sorry for them, but what do I care?"

He faced Ladd, spreading his arms wide, and made an extremely self-centered declaration:

"'Kill or be killed.' That's a phrase I've got no use for. Because, see, I'll never be killed. Remember this—"

After a moment's pause, his lips warped ominously, and he went on:

"Being a cream puff and feeling sorry for people are privileges only the strong get. And…I'm strong."

It was greater than he'd imagined. This guy made Ladd's intent to kill far stronger than he'd ever dreamed.

His tension had already dropped a level, down to its lowest line. In a voice as if he were squeezing out his hatred, Ladd spoke to the red shadow in front of him.

"Are you…one of *those* guys? Do you think you really aren't gonna die…?"

The answer he got back was just what he'd expected.

"Of course. After all, the world is mine."

The statement was so over the top that Ladd and Chané were speechless. Claire kept talking, indifferent.

"This world is mine. I think it might even be something in a long, long dream I'm seeing. I mean, think about it. You could be illusions; I can't prove you actually exist. So I figured this world revolves around me. If I believe I can do something, I'm always able to do it, and when it gets close to my time to go, I bet somebody comes up with some kind of immortality elixir. Or maybe I'll wake up from the dream I'm having now and go to some other dream. In other words, I'll last forever."

"…How? How can you think crap that's that damn self-centered?!"

"I don't have much of an imagination. I can't begin to imagine what things will be like after I'm dead. I really can't think it. I can't imagine 'nothing.' People say that once you're dead, it's dark for eternity. 'Nothing' means you wouldn't even be able to sense that darkness, see? That's what I can't imagine. I can't visualize myself disappearing. So it's, you know… In other words, in this world, there's no such thing as perfect nothingness. When guys who aren't me die, though, they disappear. I worked backward from that conclusion and came to this one. In short, I'm the only thing in this world that doesn't go away. That means the world is mine. The other guys are just dreams I'm seeing."

Ladd didn't even feel like arguing anymore. He'd concluded that this punk was completely off his rocker.

"If I had to sum it up briefly, it's this: As long as I believe I can do it, nothing is impossible for me."

At those words, Ladd's tension started to climb again, and he burst out laughing:

"I see. So that's why you're going to help the broad? Getting help from a fella like you is more of a pain than anything. Ain't that right?"

He looked to Chané for agreement, but she was silent, gazing at Claire.

On seeing this, Claire gave a little sigh and responded:

"There's one other reason I'm taking her side. If she says she'll leave the passengers alone, I won't have a reason to kill her anymore, but...you white suits are different. You're going to pay for the crime of killing Tony."

"Tony...?"

For a moment, Ladd didn't know who that was, but after he gave it a little thought, it hit him. That had been the name of the conductor Dune had dusted in order to get his uniform. He remembered seeing it on the outfit's name tag.

"...That's a contradiction, monster. Other people are just dreams, yeah? In that case, it shouldn't bother you all that much."

"Even if Tony were imaginary, what's wrong with feeling friendship or obligation toward him? If a nightmare breaks my dream, I'll erase it with extreme prejudice."

"Got a comeback for everything, don'tcha...? Argh, you make me sick as hell! Die! Die and atone! Did you butcher my pal Dune over a loony emotion like that?!"

Ladd seemed to have lost his cool completely: As he spoke, he charged headlong at the crimson catastrophe. Then he paid out several jabs at a speed no amateur's eyes would have been able to follow.

"You people killed Tony first."

Giving a perfectly natural retort, Claire warded off that attack... using a method that would ordinarily have been impossible.

"Say wha—?!"

Ladd's eyes opened wide in shock. In response to the machine gun–like exchange of jabs, Claire had flown toward Ladd. He'd literally launched himself off the roof of the train and leaped through space. Then he caught Ladd's arms with both hands and used his momentum to stop himself in a handstand, right over Ladd.

It was all Ladd could do not to fall over, and Claire took advantage of that momentary vulnerability to land behind his back.

"You little shit!"

Ladd turned around, attempting a punch as he did so, but a dry report rang out, and part of his right ear was blown away.

"?!"

He didn't even have time to groan at that moment's pain.

When he looked, Claire was standing right in front of him, holding a pistol. Quietly, with the smoking muzzle pointing at Ladd's forehead, right between his eyes, he said:

"Humiliated?"

Without waiting for an answer, Claire continued stringing words together impassively.

"I'm not so confident in my hand-to-hand skills that I think nothing beats unarmed combat. I think swords are tougher than fists, and guns are tougher than swords. I mean, it depends on the situation, but still."

Claire often used guns in his work as well, and he felt he knew more about their force and handling than the average person. And although he'd had one this entire time, he hadn't used it.

"If I'd used a gun, you'd have been dead on the spot. But I didn't use it. I thought bare hands would be enough against a nobody like you. Humiliated?"

Although there was no telling what he was thinking, Claire put the gun he'd gone to the trouble of drawing back into his coat.

"I went out of my way to shoot your ear that time, too. Humiliated?"

Ladd didn't understand what his foe was driving at. He just kept feeling humiliated, as he'd said.

"Die while you feel all the humiliation you're capable of feeling. That's how you'll make amends to Tony...or rather, to my world, for taking Tony out of it."

True, it was humiliating. There was no greater humiliation. Right now, on a completely different level from ambition and calculation, Ladd simply wanted to kill this man. He didn't need any pleasure or profit. As long as he could give the warped despot in front of him "nothing," that was enough.

When he thought this, a laugh welled up naturally.

"Ha-ha... Hee-ha-ha... Well okay then, self-proclaimed ruler of the world... How are you planning to slaughter me now? Yeah, I'm gonna prove the world sure as hell ain't gonna go the way you want it to. I'll butcher you and bury you under a ton of 'nothing'!"

At those words, Claire brooded a bit. Then, abruptly, he looked in the direction of the coupling. Grinning as if he'd hit on an idea, he spoke to Ladd:

"Before that, let me ask you something. The lady in the white dress who was with you. Is that your gal?"

Ladd was taken aback by the abrupt question, but even as he scowled, he gave a clear answer:

"She's my fiancée. What, you're planning to nitpick my girl, too?"

"No… I just thought, 'Wow, even a scumbag like you has a lady'…"

"So a homicidal maniac like me can't enjoy true love?"

In fact, their warped affection was a far cry from "true love," but Ladd spoke decisively, without hesitation.

Even as they kept up this conversation, which didn't mesh with the situation at all, Ladd's intent to kill was steadily building. At this rate, it wouldn't be long before it caught up with the murderous intent Claire was radiating. Even so, the acrobat wasn't the least bit unsettled. He simply responded to the previous moment's question.

"I see. Hearing that convinced me. I know what's going to happen to you next."

Claire's face warped cheerfully. His face was already flooded with a brutality that would have been impossible to imagine from his conductor self, and the best word to describe his smile was *vicious*.

"You're going to jump. Voluntarily. Right off this train."

As he spoke, he let his eyes shift slightly to the side. In spite of himself, Ladd followed his gaze.

When his eyes had completely turned to the side…Ladd realized that a woman's upper body was protruding from the gap between the cars, and his expression changed, dramatically and openly. The woman was wearing a white dress. It was a woman Ladd knew very well, the woman he loved best, the woman he most wanted to kill.

⇔

In the second-class compartment, the gray magician was treating Jack.

As the white-suited man helped him work little by little, he asked a question that had been on his mind:

"Say, what're those books in that bag? I can't even read the words on the covers. Are they magic books or something?"

Apparently, in his mind, the man in front of him still seemed like a magician.

"They're medical books…although I suppose they're not much different from magic books. They're written in German, so it's no wonder you can't read them."

The white suit thought—wrongly—that his lack of schooling had been ridiculed, but without caring all that much, he kept asking questions.

"And then, see… I get that you dress like that to hide all your injuries. But listen, why gray? Don't doctors usually wear white?"

"White reflects too much light. It's not suitable for use during surgeries. That said, I personally like gray, and that may be more to the point. I think gray is the best color for blending in with the world. 'Hiding' might be a better way to put it than 'blending in.'"

"Come to think of it, Lua said something like that, a long time ago. She's the doll who just left."

On hearing that, the gray magician quietly began to murmur about what he'd sensed in her.

"That girl resembles me, in a way. Her desire for death. However, something about her is fundamentally different from me. Her eyes are strikingly similar to those of a type of fellow you sometimes see on the battlefield. They're the eyes of somebody who personally wants to die but who has a precious loved one. Taken the other way around, they're the eyes of someone who's needed by someone else. I heal wounds out of sheer obligation, and compared with me, her value to this world is many times greater."

The white-suited man didn't really understand what the magician meant, but he gave him a response, anyway:

"Hey, c'mon. If a doctor like yourself has no value, then ours is definitely in the negatives… Well, it's a fact, so there's no help for it, I guess."

As the white suit muttered this, he kept on privately wondering about things it did no good to think about at this point: *Agh, why am I doing something this stupid? A train robbery… And that Ladd idiot, too: If he likes Lua, he shouldn't be pulling her into stuff like this.*

⇔

Lua had climbed up to the roof at the coupling and had finally managed to find Ladd. However, Ladd was already squaring off with the red monster.

I finally found him. I have to hurry, have to tell Ladd, before that monster kills him. We have to run, from this train, from that monster, as far as we possibly can. Ladd and I, or no, at least Ladd…

As far as Lua was concerned, Ladd was someone *necessary*. He wasn't just the person who would kill her. Even without that, at this point, she couldn't imagine a world without Ladd. Life and death were two sides of the same coin, and by killing her, he would probably find joy in living. It was a one-way cycle of reincarnation that existed only between the two of them. To Lua, who had kept expanding this delusion for herself, Ladd's death was equivalent to the world itself crumbling and disappearing. In a different way than Claire, she was a fanatic who believed in her own view of the world—a fanatic, and a martyr. The difference between her and Claire was that her world was encased in the great vessel known as Ladd.

"Lua! You idiot, I told you to go rest!"

Cold sweat broke out on Ladd's face.

Dammit, why is she there, why there, why is the monster the one closest to her?! Dammit to hell!

Claire understood what Ladd's expression meant in an instant. He took a certain object out of his coat—*I'd been wondering who to use this on*—and began examining the surrounding scenery, looking entertained. At first glance, the thing he'd taken from his coat seemed to be a simple rope, but apparently, both ends were tied into loops. The rope was like two lassos, the sort cowboys threw, put together.

"All right, remember what I said? I said you were going to jump off this train on your own."

"Lua! C'mon, get down from there and run!"

"…! ………!"

Lua was screaming something, desperately, but from where he was, he couldn't catch it. Ladd clicked his tongue, then ran at the red monster.

Even though Ladd was closing in at tremendous speed, the scarlet shadow didn't budge. He just kept unwinding the long rope he held in his hands. *This is my chance. I dunno whether this world is yours or what, but if it is, I'll just end it right along with you.*

One more step and he'd be within striking distance. At that point, finally, he heard what Lua was screaming.

"—Don't! You mustn't fight him! You'll be killed! Hurry, run—"

It's way too late, idiot. In that case, quit worrying about me and run for it, you moron.

Lua's instincts were usually right on the money. Rather than instincts, it might have been better to say that she had outstanding insight. Her instincts had saved Ladd many, many times, and he trusted her insight far more than his own instincts.

…But that was irrelevant now.

He was fully aware that this red man was real bad news. He didn't need her to tell him that.

He also knew that if they fought, he'd die.

So what? I'm gonna slaughter this guy. Even if he kills me, I'll kill 'im.

In the instant Ladd's punch was about to connect, the red shadow grinned and threw the rope. One of the loops went around Lua's neck. He threw the other toward the side of the train—and it caught on something in the midst of the racing scenery. It was a post with a hook on it, meant for collecting the mail. Claire had kept an eye on his surroundings, timing his move for that exact moment.

The interval between the two loops was like a writhing snake. The rope should have been a long one, but it was being pulled from either end, and the slack between the two loops was vanishing rapidly.

"You…unholy, black-gutted bastard!"

Ladd let the fist that had been about to hit the demon sweep right by him.

If Ladd landed his punch, he wouldn't make it in time.

Unless he jumped immediately, he wouldn't make it in time.

Unless he grabbed Lua right away, he wouldn't make it in time—

Ladd's right hand grabbed the base of the looped rope, while his left hand held Lua to him tightly.

In the next instant, the rope hit its full length, and Ladd's and Lua's bodies were airborne. An incredible shock and intense friction ran through Ladd's right hand, but he couldn't let go of the rope. The instant he let go, Lua's neck would be wrung like a chicken's. The bones in her neck would probably be gone even before that happened. Even when the heat from the friction burned his hand and the flesh began peeling off, Ladd hung on doggedly.

As the torrent of force swallowed him up, he saw the ring finger of his left hand fly off. While they fell, he'd been trying to get the rope off Lua's neck, and apparently, it had gotten tangled in a weird way.

Ah, that's one hell of an engagement ring.

As he was thinking this, his right hand began to slip on the blood. In an instant, the rope tightened, closing on Lua's neck, trying to strangle her.

The moment Ladd gave an inarticulate yell, the rope…neatly came undone and fell away.

——Huh?

The rope around her neck had been tied with a fake knot that came untied when pulled hard. It was a knot even amateurs could tie, the sort used in magic tricks. As that fact hit him, Ladd realized he'd been duped.

"That bastard *AAAAAAAAAAAAH!*"

His eyes flew open with such force his eyeballs seemed about to pop out, but it was much too late. Since his right hand had been clenched around the knot, he and Lua had ended up jumping off the train.

Their bodies flew through the air, locked in an embrace, and as the rope left them, they began drifting gently toward the ground. Even though they were falling under their own momentum, the pace at which the ground went by was abnormally fast.

When Ladd looked, Lua was struggling, trying to maneuver her own body under his. She was probably trying to protect him, even a little bit, from their impact with the ground.

Idiot. Quit doing stuff that makes no sense. Don't let your eyes come alive like that—it looks lousy on you.

You're making me want to kill you right now, mooooron.

As he thought this, his consciousness was gradually dimming.

Just when his mind seemed about to give way completely, over Lua's shoulder, he saw something rushing at them.

It was one of the many poles that stood along the tracks, a different pole from the one the rope had caught on. If nothing changed, Lua's back was certain to smash into it.

Conductor. Is this part of your "convenient world," too? Like hell. I'll show you the world ain't gonna go your way that easy—

Ladd's eyes had been nearly closed, but he opened them wide, pouring even the energy he would have used on a fighting yell into his fist. In the midst of a hot silence, he paid out a poorly executed left straight.

…Right at the pole that was racing toward them, behind Lua.

Paying no heed to the fact that his ring finger was missing, he clenched his fist and punched the oncoming pole.

The impact surged into an explosion.

The red shadow had watched the scene, and his eyes quietly narrowed in a smile. He spoke to Chané, ahead of him:

"I don't know about the guy, but the girl's safe. It looks like he protected her, right to the end. And here I thought he was just scum. That's really something, don't you think?"

Chané couldn't answer. She didn't understand this man. He was far too uncanny to make an enemy of, but she really couldn't ally herself with him, either. She gulped. Premonitions welled up in her heart, one after another: *If I fight this man, I will die.*

"All right."

The man's eyes swiveled back to her.

"I promised I'd kill whoever survived, but...we don't know whether that guy's dead. What do you think I should do?"

With an expression that seemed to say he'd seen through everything, Claire gazed into Chané's eyes. Chané felt as if the terrible radiance that seemed to absorb all light was on the verge of swallowing her whole.

"Oh, just for the record, don't think I'm a complete ogre, all right? If he hadn't gone to save her, the rope would have come untied on its own. Really, I swear."

As he thought about what to do next, Claire switched to an unrelated subject.

Now that the leader of the white suits who'd killed Tony was gone, he should probably go dispose of the black suits. So for the moment, it was clear that he'd have to do something about the woman in front of him.

"Ah, right. The Huey fella you were talking about... He's important to you, personally?"

It was an abrupt question, but Chané quietly nodded.

"Is he your lover?"

She shook her head no.

"Family?"

She nodded.

"Your father?"

She nodded.

"Is Huey your group's boss?"

She nodded.

"By the way, what do you want to do? Do you want to fight me to the death, or—"

He was about to say *run away*, but at a sudden thought, he substituted something else.

"—Or should I kill the guy who's trying to kill your family? That white suit?"

At the question, Chané's eyes widened.

"I already went and told him I'd help you out, so if I kill you or desert you now, it'll leave a bad aftertaste. I'm a hitman. Make your choice: Hire me, or fight me to the death here. Just so you know, if you don't kill me now, somebody might hire me to kill Huey later."

Those words generated great conflict in Chané's heart. She didn't understand this man. Would it be all right to trust him? The one thing that was clear to her was that he was probably stronger than anybody. That alone was solid fact.

How much did this man know? How long had he been listening to her conversation with the white suit?

Chané's heart wavered, but the next question disturbed it even more violently.

"Oh, right. That Huey guy... Is he actually immortal?"

(!)

This man, too? Is he after that as well?

Why have I been hesitating? Didn't I make up my mind long ago? Haven't I always been the only one to protect Huey, my father? Before now, and from now on?

I mustn't trust others. After all, others will always be outsiders, nothing more.

Kill the enemy. Kill only the enemy. I can protect Huey by myself; I'm enough. I won't let anyone get close. Nobody dangerous, nobody, nobody.

In the end, I'm the only family Huey has—

A cold light came into Chané's eyes.

Maybe he'd picked up on the abnormality. Claire tilted his head to the side and spoke.

"What's the matter? That's a scary face... Is this about that? Are you thinking...I might threaten Huey and steal his immortality?"

He was right on the money. The coldness in her eyes faltered, very slightly. Even as she curbed her agitation, the artless woman nodded, giving a response that was honest to a fault.

On seeing this, Claire smiled and cheerfully repeated his question: "Is Huey the only family you've got?"

The question was similar to the one she'd been asked a moment ago, but Chané answered it honestly. She'd decided that, for now, her first priority was to find some sort of vulnerability in this man.

"I see. You think you're the only one you can trust to protect Huey, since you're family...and because you think that way, you can't trust me. Right?"

That wasn't the only reason she couldn't trust others, but he wasn't wrong, so she nodded.

"Still, you want to protect Huey no matter what. Right?"

She didn't even have to think about that question. However, the instant she heard his next words, Chané's mind went blank.

"So I had an idea: If I marry you, I'll be Huey's son. That'll make him family for me, too, and in that case, problem solved."

For a moment, she didn't understand what he was saying. The more Chané thought about it, the more her mind overflowed with question marks and exclamation points.

Without even trying to confirm her answer, Claire kept talking nonchalantly.

"All right, now we've got three options instead of two: Either fight me to the death here, or hire me for a job and put me on your team even though you don't trust me, or marry me and we'll protect Huey together. Those three. Do you understand?"

She really didn't. What in the world was this man thinking?

She couldn't understand, she couldn't understand. This man, strength and personality included, was different from any human Chané had ever encountered before. Or no, maybe he really was a monster, not a human.

"Frankly, I wouldn't have minded just going with the 'marry me' and 'fight to the death' options, but that would have seemed like a threat, and I thought it would be kind of unmanly. Besides, if I did something like that, my brother Keith might actually disown me."

Chané stood, unsteadily, but she had absolutely no idea what she should do next.

She simply listened to what Claire was saying with a dazed expression.

"Oh, are you maybe thinking you wouldn't want a loveless marriage? Don't worry about that. I'll love you. Or I could let that Huey fella adopt me, if you'd like that better. In that case, we'd be siblings. Whether you'd be my big sister or my little sister depends on your age, I guess."

Even as she thought that that wasn't the problem here, Chané was still at a loss over how to respond. Right now, her top priority was carrying out Huey's rescue operation. However, this man would get in the way. That said, she probably... No, she definitely couldn't win against him.

Before Chané's brain could completely process everything, Claire abruptly put his face right up close to hers.

"Well, you can take the marriage thing as a joke if you want, but let me just go on the record as saying that I'm serious."

Then he looked right into Chané's eyes. It was as if deep holes had opened up in his eyes, and demons were beckoning to her soul from their depths.

A strange sensation ran down Chané's spine, but she couldn't resist. Right now, all she could do was listen to what Claire said.

"Unlike your comrades, I won't sell you out."

He spoke quietly, ever so quietly.

"I'd never need to, see. Tough guys, people who are stronger than anyone, never betray their comrades. There's just no sense in it. And I'm strong. Understand?"

Even with the roar of the wheels and the wind that surrounded the train, those words rang powerfully in Chané's ears.

"I also won't steal the secret of Huey's immortality, the way you're worried about. If he says he'll give it to me, sure, I'll take it, but I won't grab it away from him. I don't need to."

Then he said the words he'd said several times in the past few minutes:

"Even without the power of immortality, there's no way I'm gonna die. Because I believe I won't. So you just stay quiet and believe in me."

His eyes still radiated a deadly light, but somehow…he seemed to be smiling.

"Believe that I'm a man who'll never die."

After listening to him speak for a while, Chané seemed to have resolved to give him some sort of response.

Just as she began to move her head, a sharp shock ran through her. A red hole opened in her shoulder, and her body lurched violently.

"What?"

At that moment, Claire heard a gunshot.

A sniper, huh? Fun.

After making sure that Chané's wound wasn't life-threatening, he turned in the direction of the gunshot.

At this distance, he was close enough to see. After assuring himself of this, Claire decided to get rid of the sniper first.

"We'll hit a river soon. If you don't want the police to catch you, jump off there. Carve your response into the roof for me, all right? It looks like the other black suits are going to kill you, anyway, and you don't need to stick with the train any longer, do you?"

With that, he trained his eyes on the finger of the distant sniper. In his heart, he believed that he could see. The egotism that controlled the world poured all of Claire's nerves into his eyesight, and a clear view of Spike's finger opened up before him. The job of conductor required good eyes in the first place, but since he also sniped on occasion, both his jobs called for perfect eyesight. In order to obtain it, he'd worked hard at lots of different things, but in the end, it had also been tidied away as "talent."

"You've got eyes like mine. You don't know what to turn your emotions on, so you just store them up inside yourself. Eyes like that."

He smiled awkwardly.

"The only thing in this world I can't do anything about is my dumb, boneheaded self."

For that reason, Claire took the murderous intent generated by tragedy and various absurdities and turned it all on himself. He lived with all the killing intent his eyes radiated sealed away inside himself.

"Well, at any rate, you nicked my ear. Even if it was an accident," he told Chané. "I'm the center of the world, and you left proof that you exist on me. So you try coming over to the side that dreams—to the side that controls the world… You're welcome here."

Rubbing the wound that had been inflicted on him through the wall, he turned toward the front of the train, getting ready to launch himself into an all-out sprint.

"If you want to, you can throw a knife at my back. I'll dodge it."

With those last words, the man began to run across the roof at extraordinary speed, and before long, he disappeared over the side of the train.

After she'd watched the small shadow advance, avoiding Spike's bullets as it went, Chané brooded about something for a short while. Then she nodded as though she'd made up her mind.

Taking out a small knife that had been secured to her leg, she began using it to carve words.

On the roof of the train, she wrote her answer to the red monster.

Then, when she saw that the train was over the river, Chané quietly leaped into the air.

⟺

The train's top secret cargo: the large quantity of explosives Czes had prepared…as well as Jacuzzi and his friends, who'd boarded the train to get it.

When one of those friends—the big brown-skinned guy named Donny—saw that they'd come to the river, their designated spot, he began to throw the boxes packed with explosives down off the railroad bridge. The river was deep, and the crates' seals and packing materials were perfect. After all, if a splash like that was enough to detonate them, they wouldn't be usable in the first place. Jacuzzi's group were simple people, and based on this simple thought, Donny pitched box after box of explosives off the train, with no hesitation whatsoever.

Just when he'd nearly thrown them all, Donny saw something weird. He thought he'd seen a woman in a black dress jump from above the cargo door. In other words, from the roof of the train.

"Aah? Woman? …Nahhh, no way. Just imagination."

Donny didn't give it much thought. He just kept concentrating on throwing boxes.

$$\Longleftrightarrow$$

Nice and Nick, two of the cargo robbers, had managed to escape thanks to Rachel. When they set off warning explosions in the first-class cars, the crew members in the locomotive finally began to notice that something was wrong.

"Hey… What was that?! That blast, just now!"

"The train sorta swayed a bit."

The engineers were a pair of elderly brothers. They were hard of hearing, and their ears hadn't picked up on the earlier gunshots. But, as one would expect, the noise of Nice's warning explosions got through to them.

Bomb blasts roared out one after another.

"Step outside and take a little look-see, wouldja?"

"Me? Goldarnit…"

Just as the younger brother was preparing to go out, they heard a voice from beyond the door.

"Gramps, it's me."

It was the voice of someone they both knew: the young conductor. His face was the polar opposite of the one he'd shown Ladd and the others a short while ago: It was his conductor's face, and his eyes were gentle.

"Oh, is that Claire? Did you come all the way over the tender to get here?"

"What're you doin' here? What the heck were those explosions? Should we maybe stop the train?"

Even as they spoke, the explosions continued.

"No, Gramps. It's the other way around: Whatever you do, please *don't* stop the train."

"Huh? Whaddaya mean?"

After pulling Spike off, Claire had come to check on the engine room, just in case, and then the explosions had begun. He thanked himself for this good fortune.

With those explosions, the signal from the conductors' room wouldn't do any good. If this kept up, they'd stop the train immediately. Consequently, on the other side of the door, Claire decided to do a little acting.

"It's train robbers. They're coming after us on horseback right now and firing!"

"They're *what*?!"

"Where are they?!"

"It looks like they're staying under cover as they move! You can't really tell from here, but we'll be crossing a river soon, remember? Once we're over that bridge, they won't chase us… So don't worry, and keep the train moving."

He didn't know what the explosions really were, either, but for now, he made something up.

He couldn't let them stop the train here.

"Hnnnrrrgh, roger that! We'll run 'er at full speed. Just leave it to us!"

"What're you gonna do, huh?"

"It doesn't look like there are any injuries among the passengers yet, so I'll get them evacuated."

"I see. You be careful, you hear?"

"Thank you, sir. I'm off, then."

Without letting the old men see his face once, Claire put the locomotive behind him.

What he'd really wanted to say was *Thank you for all you've done for me up till now*, but under the circumstances, there was no help for it. He said a silent good-bye to these friends, whom he might never see again.

Even if the world does revolve around me, there are lots of people I'll always be indebted to. Dammit, if we're late getting to New York now, I'll never be able to look the Gandor brothers in the face again.

And so the train sped on.

⟺

There was no telling what sort of path Isaac and Miria had wandered, but they were currently puttering around in the third-class carriage.

"Hmm, I'm not seeing them... No white-suited fellas, and no Rail Tracer."

"Yes, they vanished! It's just like a mystery!"

Because they'd passed in front of the respective rooms while Jacuzzi held one black suit captive and Ladd was torturing another, in the end, Isaac and Miria hadn't encountered any darkly dressed trouble.

"Say, Isaac? You're sure it's okay not to check the freight room?"

"It's fine. The monster eats people gradually, starting from the back of the train. That means it won't be in a freight room that's farther back than the one that had the dead body in it!"

"But then why did you check the conductors' room so carefully?"

"Heh-heh-heh. They say the culprit always returns to the scene of the crime, you know."

"Wow, that's amazing! Isaac, you're just like Holmes!"

Rattling off examples of incoherent reasoning, they went deeper into the third-class car.

Along the way, they checked each of the rooms carefully. There were people tied up in each compartment, so they undid their ropes for them as they went.

"Oh, thank you so much! What on earth is going on?!"

The passengers they rescued all said the same thing, and each time, Isaac gave them the same answer:

"They're fighting some sort of gun battle, and a monster's walking around eating people."

Those words earned him terribly odd looks, but nobody made any attempt to go outside.

Something had occurred to them. For a while, in a nearby room, they'd heard a child's horrible screams. Then they'd heard a sound like breaking glass, and the noises had stopped entirely. Whether it was a monster or black-suited robbers, nobody felt like casually going outside.

On hearing this, Miria murmured, "Oh no. Could that have been Mary and…?" She sounded uneasy.

As the happy couple made their way through the third-class carriage, they realized that the door of the next room ahead was standing open.

Was it the monster? The pair held their breath, gulped, and approached the door with exaggeratedly stealthy footsteps.

When they quietly peeked inside, two black suits were there. They were looking out the window and whispering to each other about something. Upon seeing them, Isaac and Miria began conversing in whispers, too.

"Aha! I bet they're picking on that child!"

"Yes, they're bullies!"

"As a gunman, I can't forgive evildoers like them! Right, Miria?!"

"Yes, you're a nice-guy outlaw!"

During a certain incident a year ago, the pair had knocked out three opponents who'd been carrying machine guns. They were uncomplicated people, and no doubt this had helped them conquer their fear of guns somewhat.

That said, at the time, they'd done it by hitting the assailants with a car.

"…And so I'll challenge them to a duel!"

"No, you can't! You could die!"

Naturally, Miria tried to stop him, but Isaac's resolve was pointlessly firm.

"Even if you know you're going to die, there are some things you've just got to do. That's the samurai way!"

"Ooh, Isaac... Then I'll duel, too!"

"How do you think they got the kid down there, anyway?"

"You'd have to walk outside the train, wouldn't...?"

As the black suits were staring at Czes's body and talking to each other, something struck the backs of their heads.

"Wha—ghah...*koff, kaff*...gyagheeeee yee! ......Hee...! ...Hee..."

White powder flew around the pair, and they'd drawn in big lungfuls of it. It was the special powder Isaac and Miria always used in robberies: a blend of lime and pepper. This time, in imitation of a duel, they'd packed the powder into gloves and thrown them at the men. The black suits had inhaled it directly, and they couldn't breathe, couldn't see. They had no hope of firing their guns. All they wanted right now were hands to cover their faces, and so they couldn't hold on to a weapon.

Rationally, they knew they mustn't let go of their weapons, but they also just couldn't take it. They fumbled the tommy guns, dropping them.

When the wind from the window dispersed the lime and they finally started to feel better, what awaited the two black suits was two outlaws, pointing their own machine guns at them.

Leveling the Chicago Typewriters, the pair delivered the most unjust line imaginable:

"We challenge you to a duel!"

"Yes, we'll start when the coin hits the ground!"

Two individuals holding machine guns were challenging unarmed opponents to a duel.

"Miria, I don't have any coins."

"You're right! Say, do you have a coin?"

Miria tried asking the black suits, but Isaac hastily canceled her request:

"Miria, no! Just try borrowing a coin from these guys! If we win, we'll be skipping out on a loan! No gunman's pride would allow a thing like that!"

"Oh, yes, that's true! Let's make a noise using something else, then!"

After giving it a little thought, Isaac spoke quietly:

"Right. In that case, the sound of this machine gun will signal the start of the duel."

"Yes, that's perfect!"

Realizing that these two idiots were serious, the black suits cried and apologized and begged for forgiveness.

Having shut the black suits into the neighboring third-class compartment, Isaac and Miria returned to the room.

"All right, where's this child?"

"They were talking about something over by the window."

"I see! I bet they hung the kid upside down…"

"Meanies!"

Isaac and Miria hastily looked out the window, then found themselves speechless. What they saw was Isaac's friend. More accurately, it was the boy they'd just met, whom Isaac and Miria had arbitrarily decided was their friend. The small body that was caught beside the wheels, the tragically altered corpse that was missing its right arm and both legs, belonged to Czeslaw Meyer.

⟺

I swear, you never know what's going to end up being lucky in this world. Who'd have thought my plans for when I got nabbed by the cops or the mafia would come in handy on a train like this…

As Rachel gazed at her jagged, sharpened nail, she was grateful for the good fortune of her continued survival. Sitting down on the connecting platform between the second- and third-class carriages, she looked up at the slice of sky that was visible between the cars.

After being captured by the black suits, Rachel had taken advantage of the guards' disappearance to cut her ropes, then managed to escape by going out the window and traveling underneath the train. She'd also undone the ropes of the two others who'd been tied up there—the girl with glasses over an eyepatch and her companion—and she wondered whether they were doing all right. Unfortunately, even if Rachel was able to worry about other people, she didn't have the wherewithal to go save them now.

"Ughk..."

Fierce pain ran through her leg. It was the wound she'd gotten from being sniped when she'd saved that mother and daughter. The bullet had torn the outside of her thigh, greatly reducing her physical capabilities. For the moment, she'd managed to stop the bleeding, but she was still in severe pain.

Unless she happened to find a doctor or something, the only thing to do was rest quietly for a little while. Rachel drew a deep breath, then opened the door from the connecting platform to enter the third-class carriage. She needed to find a room without enemies and lie down...

Her irritability was growing along with her pain, and the voice that blared out behind her was all too sudden:

"D-d-don't move! You maggot!"

When she turned, she saw a familiar face.

A man with a little mustache and a face like a pig's. The man who'd been in the dining car—Rachel's sworn enemy—stood there.

In an extremely unpleasant twist, the mustachioed man held a rifle.

"Huh, what're you...? A girl?"

The man's eyes held a vague contempt, but he kept the gun's muzzle fixed on Rachel.

Although there was no way she could have known, the rifle the mustachioed man held had belonged to the white suits. The pervert Chané had killed had been carrying it; the man with the little mustache had gotten the gun from the man's corpse, which had been lying in front of a janitor's closet. Chané hadn't bothered to take the guns from all the people she'd defeated. As a result, this one was now in the mustachioed man's hands.

"Huhn! You must be with those white suits. Admit it! Oh, I know:

Everyone walking around bold as brass on this train, in this situation, is a scoundrel!"

Saying something that was, in a way, correct, the man with the little mustache edged closer to the stowaway.

After being bounced from the dining car by Isaac, Jon, and the others, he'd wandered around in abject terror. Then, just when his reason had almost reached its limit, he'd gotten his hands on a weapon. It was likely that his basic personality had a lot to do with it as well, but warped thoughts had begun to eat away at him. He'd become obsessed with the idea that he had to kill *somebody*—somebody who was trying to kill him. He'd been lurking in the car for a while now, searching for someone he thought he'd be able to do in. He'd let the terrifying man in white and the brown-skinned giant pass right by, and the woman in white had run off before he could call to her.

Now he'd finally found a sacrifice to appease his heart. Even if he understood that Rachel wasn't one of the white suits, at this point, it was probably impossible for him to simply lower his gun.

"I know. My ideas have never been wrong before. Look what a success I've made of my life, based on that conviction. There's no way in Hades I'm going to let scum like you end that for me now!"

Growing sad, Rachel looked up into empty space.

Talk about irony. I finally get an excuse to deck this guy, and he has a gun... And I've got a fresh wound in my leg.

Under the circumstances, she couldn't afford to make the man angry, but even so, she had to say something sarcastic.

"You've never been wrong? You mean that accident wasn't a mistake?"

"...?"

"The train accident. Ten years ago. You're telling me that was scheduled? You ignored the technicians' advice, and when the thing actually happened, it was all the technicians' fault? Are you saying that's right? Stuff like that? Is that really, truly what you think?"

At those words, the lunacy in the mustachioed man's eyes faded. What appeared in its place was a rational, clear intent to kill.

"You. How do you know about that? Who are you?"

Ordinarily, if he'd been confronted with the facts like this, he would probably have been able to call it nonsense and leave it alone. One person kicking up a fuss now wouldn't be enough to bring the facts to light. However, under these circumstances, where nobody was able to make calm decisions, the comment had been far too dangerous.

"To think you'd drag out my—or rather *our*—disgrace at this late date! I don't know who you are, but you really must be one of the white suits' friends. I'll tell them you were, at any rate."

Slowly, the barrel of the rifle turned to point between Rachel's eyes.

In the midst of that hopeless situation, for some reason, there was a sad smile on her face.

"You know, this may actually have been payback. Payback for having stolen all those rides, for constantly stomping all over the railway's pride."

"Stealing rides? Hunh. Scum does tend to accumulate slippery crimes."

"So at least now, at the very end, I'd like to die at the hands of the train. To be killed by somebody who gives everything in his work to the rails, as a proxy for the train itself—"

"Huh? Are you begging for your life? Either way, I work with trains, so I've got more than enough right to—"

As the man with the little mustache said this, he steadied his aim, slowly placing his finger on the trigger.

However, ignoring the mustachioed man's words and actions, Rachel yelled fiercely:

"So hurry, hurry up and kill me! Before this whiskered pig can do it! Kill me! Kill me! Red monster—no—Conductor!"

The man with the little mustache didn't understand what her words meant, and for a moment, his trigger finger hesitated.

The next instant, both the man's shoulders began to creak, setting up a terrific noise. At the same time, pain of a kind he'd never experienced slammed directly into his brain. Even without seeing his shoulders, he understood what was happening: Somebody had grabbed them from behind. When, screaming from the pain, he managed to turn his eyes to his own shoulder, he saw fingers, sunk impossibly deep into his flesh.

The reaction made him drop the gun in spite of himself. If things had gone just a little wrong, with momentum like that, it wouldn't have been at all odd for him to pull the trigger. However, luckily for Rachel, the rifle fell to the floor without spitting fire.

"Gawah… Gwaaaah, AAAaaah, ubugh!"

The sensation that assailed him seemed to have gone beyond pain and turned into nausea. Tears streamed from the mustachioed man's eyes, and something like gastric fluid was beginning to dribble from his mouth and nose.

Then, with a dull noise, both his shoulders jolted and slumped. The sheer strength of the grip had forcibly dislocated the joints.

"_____!"

Unable even to scream, the man with the little mustache lost consciousness instantly. The way he passed out made him look almost like an electrical appliance with a blown fuse, and it wouldn't have been strange for a bystander to have heard a *click*.

His body fell, hitting the floor face-first. A man stood beside it.

The conductor, bathed in the bright-red blood of his victims, was looking down at the mustachioed man, quietly.

Lowly conductors like us have it rough because of guys like this.

After successfully duping the engineers, Claire returned to the rear cars; looking through a window in the dining car revealed the passengers tying up surviving black suits. A glance at the corridor showed several white suits trussed up the same way. Apparently, while Claire's attention had been elsewhere, the situation had begun to resolve itself.

At any rate, he didn't think there had been any deaths among the regular passengers.

In order to check on that, Claire made his way back to the conductors' room one more time. But along the way he'd spotted a suspicious whiskered fat guy with a rifle and the ride-stealing girl from a little while ago.

At first, he'd watched the scene unfold from the shadows of the connecting platform, but he'd found himself getting angrier and angrier at Mr. Whiskers, so he'd decided to help the ride-stealing girl. He seemed to have made it just in the nick of time, right before the trigger was pulled. Whistling at his own excellent timing, Claire thought about what to do with the mustachioed man.

I guess I'll drop him off the train. He'll survive if he's lucky.

Casually thinking something horrendous, Claire approached, intending to pick up the man's body.

Behind him, a voice that managed to be commanding even as it shook called to him:

"No… Hold it!"

The masculine-sounding words had been delivered in a soprano voice. He turned. The ride-stealing girl stood there, holding the rifle at the ready.

"Get away from that man! Don't kill him!"

On hearing what she said, Claire's shoulders slumped, mystified.

"This is the guy who was about to kill you… And relax; I'm not going to do anything to you."

Does this woman have a personality like mine, maybe? Is she positive she can't die? If so, I can understand this contradiction, why she'd try to save her own enemy. That thought abruptly came into Claire's head, but from the look of the woman's face, that wasn't it: She'd broken out in a cold sweat.

"You're a weird one. First you tell me to kill you, then you tell me not to kill some other guy…"

"Not just him. Don't kill anybody else on this train! No more! If you're going to kill, then kill me and let that be the end of it!"

The woman in coveralls spoke vehemently. With a frown, Claire asked her a question:

"Why? Why would you go that far?"

Claire looked into Rachel's eyes. His own still held that inhuman light—and while they did scare Rachel, she answered him without flinching.

"My dad was a railroad technician. He loved trains, and so do I;

we're crazy about them! We probably like them a lot more than we like people!"

Is her dad the technician she was talking to this whiskered pig about?

Claire thought this, but he didn't say it; he just took in her words, quietly.

"And so, so, so, so! Don't sully it! Don't sully the pride of the people who built this train, or the pride of the train! Don't stain this train, or the rails, or the people, with anyone else's blood!"

Before she knew it, Rachel had begun to cry. Claire watched her, silently, but before long, he spoke softly.

"'Don't sully its pride,' huh? I never thought I'd hear that from a fare-dodger."

"Yeah, you're right. That means we're guilty of the same crime."

At her words, Claire's mouth warped hugely. Entertained and delighted, he turned his back on the ride-stealing girl.

"Murder and ride-stealing are the same, huh? Wow. You really are a strange one, lady."

At that point, finally, Rachel realized it, too: The man in front of her, the one she'd thought was a monster, was human, not so very different from herself. She really should have picked up on it when she managed to have an ordinary conversation with him, but her heart hadn't had anything like that kind of leeway. Now, because he had smiled, she'd finally managed to regain that slight composure.

"Unbelievable. For a while now, you've just kept giving me reminders… That I'm a conductor, I mean."

Muttering quietly, Claire put a hand into his coat and drew out a little scrap of paper. More than half of it was stained red.

"It's a ticket. Take it. Your name isn't on the passenger list, but tell 'em the conductor must have made a mistake, and stick to your guns. Nobody's going to object. Oh, and keep quiet about my being the conductor, all right?"

Letting the scrap of paper flutter to the floor, he began to walk away, deeper into the car.

"You're a pretty amazing lady, too, you know that? If I hadn't met the girl with the knives, I might have fallen for you instead. Well, if it's meant to happen, we'll probably meet again."

As he said something incomprehensible, his back got farther and farther from Rachel.

"H-hang on a minute."

"Don't worry. It looks like I won't have to kill anybody else. The only people I killed were black suits and white suits. I haven't laid a finger on the passengers. That would have been putting the cart before the horse."

"Liar! You—just a little while ago, that kid—"

When she'd gotten that far, Rachel realized something. If she remembered right, that boy had been tied…just under this car.

The moment she stopped speaking, Claire spoke as if he'd remembered, too.

"Ah! Right, that's right. I forgot. No, his situation's a bit complicated. Agh, what a pain; just ask the guy in person, would you?"

"What are you talking about?! That kid's long d…"

Ignoring Rachel's words, Claire pulled open a nearby door. It was the door of the room where he'd tortured Czes a short while earlier. And what he saw inside was—

"Waaaaaaah! Isaac, are you okay?"

What he saw was a woman in a bright-red dress, leaning more than halfway out the window.

⇔

Beside the wheels, with the cold wind eating away at his body, Czes's thoughts went by vacantly.

I wonder what's going to happen to me.

The pain that red monster inflicted on me was completely new. And sometimes it was terror instead of pain. He pared my eyeball away little by little with the long scalpel, slit my arteries, blew hard into the wounds, did the same thing to my veins. That was only the beginning. The pain he gave me after that… I can't remember it. All I can remember was that he had caused me terrible pain, and no matter how I try, I can't remember the specifics. It's not that I don't want to remember, but that I truly can't.

I may already have gone mad. If so, things went exactly as that thing planned. Is this retribution? Is it punishment for attempting to kill the people in the dining car, or punishment for evil I did in the past? I don't care which it is anymore. I just want it all to go away.

…Come to think of it, that's impossible, isn't it…? Ah, I see. Is this retribution for having lived this long, for having gone against the logic of this world, for having gained immortality? I acquired immortality so that I could be happy, but this is the result? I was given betrayal first, then loneliness, and finally terror. Is this retribution? Retribution for having eaten my companion…?

It's gotten noisy up above. Who is it now? Has he come back? That red monster? Will he inflict more of that pain on me? —Please, no.

No, nononono, anything but that, nonono, stop, I'm begging you, nononono, save me, somebody, anybody, save me, nonono—

The pain didn't come. Regaining a little of my composure, I surrendered my body to silence again. *It doesn't matter who's up there. If I can get by without being hurt, I don't care who they are.*

Even opening my eyes is too much trouble. How wonderful it would be if, when I opened them, everything up till now had been a dream. *That's it—this must be a dream. If I open my eyes, I'll still be on that tall ship.*

I'm sure the things he did were all dreams, too, and Szilard eating our companions was a dream—

A drop of some sort of liquid fell on my cheek.

Ah, so this really is a dream. Spray from the waves just struck my cheek. All right, I'll open my eyes. I'm still a child, and if I don't wake early, they'll all make fun of me—

When I opened my eyes, there was reality. Before I had time to despair, a voice came down to me from above.

"Aah! Miria, his eyes opened! He's alive! He's still alive!"

What I saw was the face of that weird gunman. He was leaning far out of the window, hanging nearly upside down, peering into my face. He seemed to have scratched his hand on the windowsill; blood was trickling from it. Apparently, one of the drops was what had struck my cheek.

What is this? What on earth is this man trying to do?

"Just hang on! Help has arrived!"

Help? Help for who? He can't mean...for me?

What is he doing? Why would he do something that pointless? Why does he have to do a thing like that for someone he just met? I don't get it. I really don't get it. If I were an old friend or a family member, or a lover, then I could see it. But a stranger he just met today? Why—?

What's this? The blood on my cheek, this guy's blood... It's trembling?

What could it mean? No, this isn't right. This is a completely different sort of motion from the wind or the vibration of the train. The blood is moving as if each drop is a living creature with a will of its own. It can't be, it can't be, no!

Ah, how can this be? Ah, ah, how can this be?! It can't be, it can't be, not these loonies, not them, it can't be! It's not true! And here, *of all places, at this worst of all possible times!*

My denial was in vain: The blood was flowing back up into the hand of the man before me. The cut on his hand was closing before my very eyes! I was sure of it: The man had not come to help me.

This man, this immortal...

He'd come to eat me.

Isaac leaned out even farther and finally went out the window entirely. Miria desperately supported his legs, but with her strength, it was a pretty impossible task. Isaac braced his hands on the wall's ornamentation, reducing the burden on Miria. Then, finally, he managed to grab the iron framework between the wheels.

Cautiously, taking care not to step on Czes or get caught up in the wheels, he crawled under the train.

"What's this?! Your arm's tied up! Hold on, I'll get that rope off you right away—"

You fool. You could have just eaten me before you set me free. The moment you untie the rope, you're finished. My right hand will—
Then Czes realized it. This time, he really did despair.

His right hand had been ground off by the red monster, and it wasn't part of his body now.

"Great! The rope's undone!"
Stabilizing his own body with his legs and left hand, Isaac cradled Czes's body with his torso so he wouldn't fall. Then, as he tried to get a firm grip on Czes with his right hand—

Smack.

Czes knocked Isaac's outstretched right hand away with his own left.

The force made him start to slip away from Isaac, and he fell from the train.

Take that! Now you won't be able to eat me—
Saying this, Czes grinned, but then his eyes flew wide open again.

He was concentrating to the limit, and to his eyes, the scene seemed to unfold in slow motion.

When Isaac realized that Czes had fallen, he had no time to think. If he'd been calm, he might have hesitated to do what he did next.

However, his head wasn't put together well enough to think of his own life under circumstances like these.

In the next moment—without a single thought, in order to save Czes, Isaac had launched himself into space.

No! Does he want my knowledge that badly?!
Isaac's right hand closed in on Czes's falling body.

It's over. This man is going to eat me, right now. Someone is going to see those damnable memories! I can't stand it, help me, somebody, anybody, I don't care who, just save me, stop, please, please, stopstopstop—

With a child's scream, Czes squeezed his eyes shut.

However, Isaac's right hand never reached his head.

Realizing that the impact of being dashed to the ground had been much softer than he'd anticipated, Czes gingerly opened his eyes.

"Eeeeeeeek! Isaaaaaaac!"

He heard Miria's scream from the window, and there was something like a wall right in front of him.

Realizing it was Isaac's clothes, at that point, for the first time, Czes understood that Isaac was holding him.

Isaac was holding on to the train with just his left hand and was being dragged.

"Ga-ga-ga-ga-ga-ga-ga-ga-ga-ga-ga!"

Giving a weird yell, Isaac desperately struggled to withstand the vibrations that were traveling up through his legs. The spurs on the heels of his western boots creaked, bouncing along over the ground. Naturally, they couldn't spin properly on the gravel, and acting as simple protrusions, they only made Isaac vibrate that much harder.

The spurs' original purpose was to control the speed of a horse, but the ground that rushed past with the force of angry waves didn't slow at all.

That said, luckily, none of Isaac's limbs were directly touching the ground. If he used both hands, he could probably manage to climb back into the train somehow. However, he refused to let go of Czes.

His left hand gradually reached its limit, and his fingers were moments from slipping off.

"Isaac!"

Miria grabbed his hand. She'd also leaped out the window without giving it any thought, descending to the wheels more skillfully than Isaac had.

However, her arms weren't strong enough, and no sooner had she caught him than she fell, too.

Even so, Miria wouldn't let the two of them get away from her. She hugged Isaac, shielding Czes's body. In that instant, Isaac took his right hand from Czes, and in a lightning-fast move that was almost like a gunman's, he threw the lasso he'd had on his back.

However, after all, he was a *gunman*, and his cowboy act didn't go well: The rope wandered through the air without catching on anything.

The three of them were dashed to the ground, struck it with tremendous force, and bounced once. Even then, Miria didn't let go of Isaac. Isaac didn't let go of Miria or the rope. Czes was protected between them, jolted by an impact that had been reduced to an astonishing extent.

Just when they thought it was all over, the end of the rope caught on something... Or rather, it *was* caught.

By the hand of some unknown person who'd reached out from under the train.

It had all happened in an instant.

Rachel had circled around under the train and had spotted Isaac and the others clinging to the metal fittings by one hand. She'd reached out to catch that hand, but she'd been a moment too late, and they'd fallen under the train. However, at the same time, something had flown from Isaac's body, and Rachel had involuntarily caught it.

It was the loop of Isaac's lasso, and its end was tied to the belt around his waist.

The next moment, unbelievable force came to bear on her arm. On the other end of the rope, Isaac and the others had hit the ground and had begun to be dragged over the gravel.

"Ugkh!"

Even if one of them was a child, Rachel's arm was supporting the weight of three people. She tried desperately to pull them in, but she really couldn't.

Would they fare better if she released them, instead of continuing to drag them like this? The thought did cross her mind, but under the circumstances, if she rashly let go, the rope might tangle in the wheels and turn the three of them into mincemeat. In the very worst case, the train might even derail. She really couldn't let go, no matter what, but—

Cruelly, her injured leg sent fierce pain through her nerves, and on reflex, she flung the rope away.

"Aaaaaaaaaah—!"

In spite of herself, Rachel screamed.

A red shadow passed right over her.

Claire was once again nimbly running along the side of the train, on the ornamentation.

It was just as he'd done on the dining car, but even faster.

Even as Rachel cried out, he reached for the end of the lasso that floated in the air.

However, his hand fell a little short. Just when Rachel thought, *It's over*, Claire launched himself off the wall. His body separated from the train completely, and in exchange, he managed to catch the end of the lasso.

Before she even understood what had happened, before her very eyes, Claire's body rotated dramatically.

No sooner had he stretched his legs out in the opposite direction from the train than one of the poles beside the tracks rushed toward him.

It's going to hit him, she thought, but in the very next instant, Claire's feet *touched down on the side of the pole.*

After a moment's pause, his body began to lean, obeying gravity.

He immediately kicked the pole, leaping back into the air.

The red figure showed up very well against the dim sky. There was even a sort of beauty about it.

Then Claire was clinging to the side of the train again, at a spot a good distance behind his original location. From his face, you'd have thought absolutely nothing had happened. In fact, it was likely that absolutely nothing had. As far as he was concerned, he'd merely done something he believed he could do. He probably hadn't thought falling was a possibility or felt even the slightest fear of death.

If it had been just Czes, he wouldn't have gone out of his way to do something like that, but the weird gunman couple were genuine passengers. They might be Czes's accomplices in crime, but thinking about that could wait until after he'd saved them. On that thought, he'd simply launched himself into space to protect the safety of his passengers.

Claire began to run with the rope, heading for the door beside him—the cargo door of one of the freight cars.

For some reason, that door was wide open, and there was a big brown-skinned figure standing in it.

⟺

Donny was bored.

They'd finished crossing the river, and he'd thrown all the cargo they were after out the side door. He'd kept back one small box packed with grenades, the way Jacuzzi had told him to, but Nice had just taken that away as well. She'd said she and Nick were going to look for Jacuzzi, so Donny was the only person still here.

With nothing to do, he'd been gazing out the open window, but...

"Hey, you! Big guy! Gimme a hand!"

Abruptly, somebody called to him. When he looked in the direction of the voice, he found himself looking outside the train.

A bright-red figure was clinging to the side of the train, right by the door.

"Ah, ahh! Y-you Rail Tracer?"

That was a word Claire had never expected to hear from this big man. For just a moment, he looked surprised, but he immediately collected himself and began to act.

Just when he'd been thinking that hauling them up by himself was going to take time, he'd discovered this giant. He'd spoken to him, simply thinking there was no reason not to use him. However...

"Never mind, just hold this! Then haul on it as hard as you can! Thanks!"

Donny was bewildered; he didn't know what was going on. Abruptly, though, farther down the train, at the end of the rope, he realized he could hear somebody screaming.

When he looked, he saw that someone was being dragged along at the end of the rope.

"Muguah, this emergency."

On seeing this, he involuntarily grabbed the rope that had been held out to him. A powerful shock ran through his body, dragging him toward the outside. Donny grabbed the edge of the door, bearing up under the strain, and then he discovered who was hanging on to the end of that rope.

The gunman duds and red cantina dress were unmistakably Isaac's and Miria's.

"Aah, this bad. I save you! Nugaaaah!"

No sooner had he spoken than, without thinking, Donny hauled on the rope with all his might. As a result—

"Whoaaaaaaaaaaaaaaaaaaaaaaaaaaa!"

Isaac and the others, who'd been dragged along the ground, leaped into the air, flew over the roof, and fell down the other side of the train.

They had no idea that the rope that stretched taut when they did this brought Jacuzzi, who was fighting on the roof, a shot at victory.

⟺

"Hey, we're over the river. Wonder if we got away from them bandits."

"Okay, better start slowin' down! The train's gonna poop out!"

The pair in the engine room raised their voices, and the speed of the train gradually slowed.

As it did so, fragments of meat began to catch up with the train.

…The red bits of meat that had been part of Czes's body: his legs and right arm.

⟺

When, with great difficulty, Isaac and the others finally managed to climb up to the top of the freight car, they rolled onto the roof and lay there.

"Thank God, we're saved!"

"Yes, saved!"

They wanted to keep lying right where they were, but they couldn't: There was a boy in pain between them, a boy who'd lost his arm and legs.

"All right, let's go! Are you okay, Czes?!"

"Hang in there!"

The pair roughly shook the badly injured boy. Czes's blood-starved brain was jostled nicely, and he felt his consciousness begin to fade again. Then the pair tried artificial respiration and chest compressions over and over, but none of it proved to be a fundamental solution.

Just then, the sound of an explosion roared from the cars behind them.

"What's that? Enemies?!"

"Look! There's someone over there!"

On top of the very end of the train, two figures clashed, and one of them vanished from the roof. Immediately afterward, an explosion that was different from the earlier one echoed, and great flames rose behind the train.

Ordinarily, the two of them would have started to kick up a racket at that point, but now wasn't the time. They were worried about Czes, but they'd also noticed the swarm of red meat fragments closing in on them, over the roof.

"Waugh! Something's coming! Something red is coming!"

"Eeeek! I-I bet it's the Rail Tracer! That must be the red monster they were talking about!"

Even as they made a ruckus, the meat fragments crawled over the roof of the car, bounding across the coupling, steadily bearing down on Isaac and the others. The red, jellylike substance kept marching like an army of insects.

"Hey, Miria! Those things are swarming Czes!"

They tried to carry Czes and run away, but the fragments kept homing in on the body of the boy who was their host.

"This is awful! They're going to eat the parts of Czes they didn't eat earlier, I just know it!"

"Dammit! As if we'd let that happen!"

Isaac covered Czes with his body, trying to protect the boy from the approaching red fragments. Miria flung herself on top of them, attempting to protect them both from the bits of meat.

The fragments didn't even seem to register that obstacle; they slipped through the gaps between their bodies. In the rising sun, the shapes of the three bodies, covered in red meat fragments, harmonized strangely.

After a short silence, the sound of a tremendous explosion brought them back to themselves. Ironically, they'd been brought to their senses by the noise of the explosives Czes himself had made.

"...Huh? The red stuff's gone."

"Yes, it disappeared... How's Czes?"

When the pair timidly peeked under their own bodies, Czes was solidly there.

...All of him, complete with his right arm and both legs.

Czes's mind had never fully shut down, although it had been a close thing. During that interval, he'd felt something he'd thought he'd lost forever.

He was sure now that neither Isaac nor Miria knew a thing about immortality. They had apparently become immortal through a coincidence of some sort. From the fact that, although they'd fallen off a train, there wasn't a scratch on either of them, it seemed likely that Miria was an immortal as well.

Right now, they were both defenseless. It would be easy for him to set his right hand on their heads. However, he really didn't want to. On seeing that he was fine, they were elated, almost in tears. Czes couldn't bring himself to eat people like them.

He had no intention of pretending to be a good person this late in the game. It was only that, if he looked into their hearts... If he shared their memories and compared them to his own mind... If he did that, then this time, Czes truly wouldn't be able to forgive himself. Living with feelings like those, forever... That would be terribly painful.

He thought it would hurt far, far more than the pain the red monster had inflicted on him.

Isaac and Miria were crying and rejoicing over the fact that Czes was all right.

"Oh, that's great! That's really fantastic!"

"Yes, it's great! But why did Czes's injuries get better?"

"That's simple, Miria."

"Why?"

Isaac had regained his usual rhythm, and he responded with absolute confidence in his answer.

"Listen, the Rail Tracer eats bad little kids, remember? I bet after he ate Czes, he realized he was really a good kid, so he came to give back what he'd eaten!"

"I see! Yes, that makes perfect sense!"

"No."

It was Czes himself who'd raised an objection to the delighted pair. However, he wasn't arguing about the reason he'd regenerated.

"I'm not a good kid... I lied."

"You lied?"

"I said I was going to New York to meet my family, but I'm really just going to see a friend."

After a little silence, Czes went on:

"I don't have a family. I didn't before—"

He was about to say, *And I never will,* but before he could, Isaac and Miria cried out:

"Is that right!"

"You really are a good boy, Czes!"

"Huh...?"

Czes was bewildered, but Isaac and Miria moved the conversation forward all on their own.

"To think you lied like that to keep everyone from worrying about you...even though you're the one who's hurting the most."

"Yes, you're a really strong, good kid, Czes!"

Without giving Czes a chance to argue, Isaac confidently thumped his own chest.

"All right! Just leave everything to me!"

"Lucky you, Czes! If you leave it to Isaac, you won't need to worry about a thing!"

Miria nodded firmly, gently patting Czes's cheek.

"So, listen, it's okay to smile!"

⇔

Claire stood quietly on the roof. The morning sun was at his back, and he was gazing at the man and woman in front of him.

The things the guy with the tattooed face was holding were probably the new explosives Czes had mentioned.

Apparently, that big man had been dumping the car's hidden cargo into the river. Claire had been wondering whether to collar him for it when he'd remembered what Czes had said:

—"*Selling explosives to the Runoratas*"—

In other words, that cargo was packed with weapons for the Runorata Family. If it disappeared, the war might turn in the Gandors' favor.

At that thought, Claire had decided to turn a blind eye to Donny and the others. *Either way, there's no way I'm letting the train run with something that dangerous onboard.* —That thought had crossed his mind as well.

And now, here was the boss of the robber gang, in the flesh. The guy with the tattooed face was running at him with a firm resolution in his eyes.

Claire already knew what he was planning to do.

He was probably attempting to slay the monster. The monster known as the Rail Tracer.

He was doing it to save the train. He'd picked this up, in a vague way, by thinking about previous situations and conversations.

The guy stood right in front of him, gazing straight into Claire's eyes. He was meeting *Claire's* eyes, right now, without showing the smallest sign of fear. *Ah, what terribly gentle eyes. He's got the eyes of a pushover. He has a tattoo like a devil, he's on a living hell of a train, and he has stronger, kinder eyes than anyone.*

Abruptly, those eyes struck Claire as unbearably beautiful. If

Claire's own eyes were like mirrors that trapped all light inside themselves, this guy's eyes seemed to hold a quiet ocean.

Just about then, behind Claire, the sun was beginning to rise. The light reflected into the young guy's face, and it felt as if even that sunlight was being absorbed into Claire's eyes.

I hate to admit it, but his eyes are much stronger than mine. They're the eyes of some hero straight out of a story. The eyes of a hero who slays monsters. If I take in a light this strong, my eyes might burst and vanish.

As he was absently thinking things like this, Claire decided to let the guy defeat him. He was the Rail Tracer. He had to disappear in the morning sun, just like the legend said. That was the duty of someone who'd told a story and pulled other people into it.

He took the body blow, and they rolled, tangling together.

Then they both fell down the side of the train.

As they fell, the young tattooed guy pulled the pin from one of his grenades. At that, for the first time, Claire spoke to him:

"Ready to go out in a blaze of glory? I don't like that."

"—Huh?"

Hugging the startled lad to him, Claire stopped himself on the side of the train. He didn't know how many times he'd done it that night, but he was tired of hooking his legs between the wheels. Maybe he'd think up some other way next time.

While he thought this, Claire spoke to the youth:

"If you don't throw that away fast, the girl up there is going to die, too."

The tattooed guy startled, then hastily flung his cargo onto the tracks. The clay was highly resistant to impacts, and the live grenade rolled over and over on the gravel—

An explosion, and then a shock wave.

Still holding the inkhead, Claire made it through the blast without any trouble.

After the wind from the blast had settled down, Claire traveled along the side, carrying the tattooed guy, then entered the conductors' room through the door in the side of the train.

He passed through the blood-soaked conductors' room, then set the young guy down on his feet in the corridor. There, Claire muttered the rest of what he'd started to say a moment ago.

"Only idiots think about going out in a blaze of glory before they start fighting. First you try fighting, and if it feels like you're probably not gonna make it, *then* you think that. Not before."

Grumbling, Claire gave the young guy's wounds a once-over. He'd been shot in the legs, but if he was able to stand, he was probably all right. Coming to an irresponsible conclusion, he gave him what was, in a way, appropriate advice:

"In Room Three of the second-class compartments, there's a guy in gray who looks like a magician. That guy's a surgeon. Have him take a look at you."

"B-but…"

"Don't worry. The loon in the white suit and the scary doll in black are gone. I think the one you took out was the last one, so relax and get some sleep."

As he spoke, Claire toyed with the item he held in his right palm. It was one of the grenades made with the new explosives. When the tattooed guy had flung all of his away, Claire had deftly caught the one that hadn't had its pin removed.

"It's fine. Just go. And don't forget about the girl up there."

The guy's tattoo warped as if he was confused, but he nodded to Claire once, politely, then went back to the train's connecting platform. He was probably planning to climb up to the roof again from there.

As he watched the young guy go, Claire said just one thing to his receding back:

"Don't keep girls waiting. Once they go off somewhere, nothing's harder to find again."

Those words were partly directed at himself.

After watching the young tattooed guy until he'd vanished, Claire twisted the stopper on the grenade and removed the fuse.

"Judging from that explosion, this should do it."

He sprinkled a decent amount of the explosives it held over the faceless corpse. He didn't need to blast it to smithereens. He only needed to make it possible to mistake the corpse for himself. Leaving it like this, with just the face ground off, made him feel highly insecure. Hopefully the forensics officers would be dimwits.

He'd make it so that Claire Stanfield had died today. That would make the next job easier as well. Harboring such calculations, Claire took out the middle-aged conductor's pistol.

"...Ah. I'm not sullying the train or anything. This is my way of saying good-bye."

Making excuses to an individual who wasn't there, he aimed the gun at the powder he'd scattered over the floor and fired.

$$\Longleftrightarrow$$

"Czes!"

When Isaac's group returned to the dining car, the Beriams were waiting there.

"Oh, you're all right! Isaac and Miria were with you, weren't they!"

"I'm so glad! I'm so, so glad you're okay, Czes!"

As he looked at the young girl who clung to him innocently, Czes had very mixed feelings. How could children open their hearts to people so easily? Of course, there were children who didn't, but the difference was an extreme one.

Oh. I suppose Isaac and Miria may be like children, too.

The sight of Mary's smile made Czes feel relieved, somehow.

He was really glad he hadn't killed the people in the dining car. Glad he'd managed to get by without betraying this child.

At the time, he couldn't fathom why he was glad about that.

Although his expression still hadn't returned, Czes said just one thing to her: "I'm sorry."

$$\Longleftrightarrow$$

Up on the now-deserted roof: The figure that came to stand there wasn't a human being. It was a single Rail Tracer that had caught up with the train.

He'd just blown up the two corpses dressed like conductors and had returned to the roof.

The message was near where Chané had been sitting.

It had been carved directly into the roof of the train with a knife.

I'll be waiting in Manhattan. I'll wait for you forever. Please, please look for me. I'll look for you as well.

On seeing it, the red monster heaved a sigh.

"Manhattan. That's great, but…for a rendezvous spot, it's way too vague. Same goes for the time… And anyway, I didn't tell her my name, and I didn't get hers… I think that white suit called her 'Chané' or something, but…is it her real name? Dammit, looking for her really *is* going to be a pain."

Gazing at the smoking conductors' room, Claire smiled a bit self-consciously.

"Besides, seriously, I can't tell from this. —I mean, is she planning to hire me, marry me, or kill me?"

Taking another long, hard look at the words, Claire rolled his shoulders, wrapping up his soliloquy.

Still… She writes a lot more politely than I expected. She might be an unexpectedly ladylike girl. Or did she fall in love with me at first sight or something? Man oh man… Would that make this a first love letter, then? Depending on the response, I think I'd like to keep this roof as a souvenir.

Arbitrarily building up his expectations for a woman he'd just met, he descended to the connecting platform.

"Sure, I'll look for you. It'll have to wait until after I've done my duty by the Gandor brothers, but…"

He wasn't muttering to himself. He was talking to the distant Chané.

"I will. Count on it."

*   *   *

And then the monster vanished.

The Rail Tracer was no more.

Everyone believed in the monster, and as in the legend, it disappeared in the morning light.

No one watched it go. It simply dissolved into the rising sun.

Express—The End

EPILOGUE II

THE WOMAN IN COVERALLS

After that, the *Flying Pussyfoot*'s journey continued without incident, and it neared the area in Manhattan in which steam engines weren't allowed.

At this point, they would be switching the lead car for an electric locomotive and—smokeless and clean—would head for Pennsylvania Station. However...

Waiting for them at the switch point was a veritable horde of police officers.

The train was immediately occupied by the police. Ironically, they did it much more briskly and efficiently than either the black suits or the white suits had.

Subsequently, the surviving black suits and white suits on the train were marched away, and after a two-hour investigation, the passengers were released. Finally, they were told that they would be generously compensated by the train's sponsor, the Nebula Corporation, on the condition that they were to speak of this incident to no one. For some reason, the government and the corporation didn't seem to want the incident to become public knowledge.

Rachel's ticket was half-dyed with blood, but the police and the station employees seemed to accept that the blood was her own.

Ironically, it was an excuse she was able to use precisely because her leg was injured.

They'd finished the first aid treatment for her shot-up leg, and with nothing to do, she was sitting in a chair when a man with a dignified air approached her.

"I hear you helped my wife and daughter. You have my thanks."

At first, she had no idea what was going on, but apparently, this was the husband of the mother Rachel had saved. In other words, he was Senator Beriam. Even though she was a low-level worker at an information brokerage, she hadn't picked up on Mrs. Beriam's identity until after she'd saved her. As she listened to him, thinking she still had a lot to learn, she was abruptly handed a thick paper envelope.

When she looked inside, it held a bundled stack of hundred-dollar bills.

"There. That's yours."

"Wha…?!"

Senator Beriam turned his back on Rachel and walked away. He hadn't even asked her name.

It wasn't as if she didn't need the money, but this was just too infuriating. It felt as if he thought she'd done what she did in order to get a reward, and Rachel flung her hand up, preparing to lob the money at his back.

However, someone gently clasped that hand. It was Mrs. Beriam herself.

"My husband's been very rude to you. Even so, please do take that money from him."

"*You* don't have to apologize."

"No, it's all right—he's clumsy, that's all. Money's the only way he knows to express his gratitude. It often causes misunderstandings, but…"

She couldn't very well throw the money at him after hearing something like that. She wanted to tell her she shouldn't have married that sort of guy, but she kept the words shut away inside.

"Besides, I really should have been the one to say it first. I truly can't thank you enough."

At that, Mary peeked out from behind the woman and thanked Rachel as well. The girl had been very shy earlier, but as she looked at Rachel now, her eyes were shining openly.

"Miss Rachel, really, thank you very much! I'm going to be as good a person as you are!"

On hearing what this slightly precocious girl said, Rachel finally felt uncomfortable. The fact that she'd been stealing a ride made her feel as if she was tricking the girl, and it pricked her conscience.

After that, in the end, she did take the money. Once they reached Pennsylvania Station, she went straight to the ticket window. After giving it a little thought, she took half the money from the envelope and bought as many tickets as she could. Then she took her bushel of tickets and left the station.

She'd already decided how she was going to spend the other half of the money. For now, in order to get her leg treated properly, she set off for a local surgeon's. The pain was the same as ever, but she walked firmly, as if she'd been set free from something.

EPILOGUE
COSTUMED BANDITS

New York   Pennsylvania Station

The doors of the train opened, and the passengers were finally released from their long, turbulent journey.

They hadn't been able to send on the cars that had served as the stage for the incident as they were, and so a different train had taken them to Pennsylvania Station.

Shadows stood on the lively, bustling platform, quietly searching for the people they were waiting for:

Firo and Ennis, waiting for their friends Isaac and Miria.

Maiza, waiting for Czes, his old colleague.

And the three Gandor brothers, who were waiting for a hitman who happened to be a family member—Claire Stanfield.

The people they were waiting for didn't appear, and the figures exiting the train were growing few and far between.

Finally, a woman in coveralls with an injured leg disembarked.

After her came an individual dressed in gray from head to toe, and a man who seemed to be his assistant. Then a guy with a tattoo on his face, a girl with an eyepatch and glasses, and a big guy who was over six feet tall.

Their eyes were drawn to the odd group, just a little, but Firo and the others kept right on waiting.

Then, the very last ones to emerge from the train were—

*   *   *

—A western gunman in badly torn clothes, and an equally tattered dancing girl.

"Hey! Ennis and Firo and Maiza! It's been a long time, my good people!"

"Yes, you look well. I'm so glad!"

At Isaac and Miria's voices, the party felt relieved, but they did get in an apt verbal jab:

"What's with those clothes?"

"Heh-heh, right now, I'm a western gunman! Call me the Belle Starr of the East!"

"But you just said you were western…"

"Wasn't Belle Starr a broad?"

Ignoring Firo and Berga's comebacks, Miria also introduced herself with a random outlaw's name:

"Okay, then I'm—! I'm the Edgar Watson of the North!"

"Uh, that's the guy who shot and killed Myra Maybelle Shirley… aka, Belle Starr."

"Whaaaaaat?! I'm going to kill Isaac?! Oh no, I couldn't stand that!"

"Nah, it's all right, Miria! I can die for you!"

Seeing that the pair hadn't changed a bit, Firo and Ennis smiled, as if relieved.

"Gah-ha-ha! You guys are as dumb as ever."

At Berga's jeer, the two flung their arms into the air and protested. The way they waved their arms around made them look like wind-up toys.

"*What?!* Make fun of me if you want, but I won't let you make fun of Miria!"

"You can make fun of me, but don't you dare badmouth Isaac!"

"In other words, we've got enough anger for two here!"

"And two people times two is four people!"

"In a majority vote, we'd win!"

"Yes, it's one against four!"

"Huh? Hold it, wait a sec…"

In response to their absurd, rapid-fire logic, Berga began folding fingers down, muttering under his breath.

"That's embarrassing, Berga. Stop."

While this was going on, Isaac cried out as if he'd remembered something:

"Oh, that's right! We've got a present for you, Ennis!"

"A really good one!"

"What, you do?! Thank you very much!"

Ennis thanked them happily. Isaac and Miria turned their backs on her and, for some reason, boarded the train again. Before long, as the group watched, mystified, Isaac came back, accompanied by the "present."

At his right hand stood a boy who'd changed clothes.

As Firo and the others looked on, wide-eyed, Isaac and Miria introduced him. They seemed truly delighted. Apparently, they'd been concerned about that letter this whole time. The one they'd gotten from Ennis in California.

"This boy is Czes!"

"Take him as your little brother, Ennis! That'll be perfect!"

EPILOGUE
ALCHEMIST

Ah, there's Maiza, right in front of me. The man who summoned the demon, the one who knows everything about immortality. That's right: I came to this city to eat this guy. What a fool. I bet he thinks I'm still who I used to be. That'll be his undoing.

All right, Maiza's close enough now. This is it: Scream "You fool!" at him and put out your right hand.

"Maiza…"

Uh… Huh? That's strange. No, that wasn't what I was going to do; why did I call his name?

Stop it, Maiza. Don't pat my head. I'm over two hundred years old already. Dammit, Maiza, I know you're right-handed. Why are you using your left hand? Don't be considerate when nobody asked you to, blast it.

Squeeze those words out: Scream "You fool!" and thrust your right hand out at Maiza!

"I missed you."

No, it's "You fool"! Dammit, pull yourself together! Just how many times do you think you've fooled people who looked like adults, and been fooled yourself?! Trust no one! You know Maiza's probably planning to eat you, too; he'll start gnawing away at you, just like that guy did! Dammit! Dammit! It's their fault! That red monster and this weird gunman couple drove me insane! But, no   Say "You fool!"   He's different   I missed him   Stop it   I was always alone   I was always lonely   No, I wanted to be alone. Say "You fool!"   I wanted to see him. Somebody from the past   No—   Put your right hand—

—I wanted to see somebody, anybody; I just wanted to see someone who knew who I was back then. To meet someone who knew me then. I just wanted to dream, to dream about that time, back on the ship, before I knew anything.

"Maiza. I missed you, Maiza!"

Tomorrow, I'm sure I'll wake from this dream, and I'll go back to being my spiteful, cunning self. However, I'll probably never think about eating Maiza again. I know if I did that, I wouldn't be able to see anything but nightmares anymore. Right now, I only want to stay in this dream, just a little longer. I want to cry, clinging to someone who knows who I used to be, just a little longer, just a little longer.

Just a little more, a little longer...

On the station platform, a young-looking immortal huddled into the chest of his old friend and cried, and cried, and cried.

On and on.

EPILOGUE
THE RAIL TRACER

"Excuse me, sir. Are you Mr. Gandor?"

"I am. What is it?"

A station employee approached Luck and handed him a single envelope. After they read its contents, Keith and his two younger brothers left the station.

When they did, on his way out, Berga apologized to Firo:

"Sorry, Firo. It sounds like Claire's waiting outside. We'll be back."

The man was waiting in the corner of an alley.

"Claire, you're the conductor. What're you doin' out here?"

"I'm not Claire anymore."

Ignoring Berga's question, he just spoke about himself, briefly.

"All right, let's go. Who should I kill first? I only managed to get a little light exercise last night, and I'm feeling rusty. I want to do a job where I can go all-out for once."

Saying this, Claire—who'd changed clothes—took the lead and started walking. Keith and the others were mildly appalled, but they followed him and set off down the alley.

"Let's get this finished up fast. I've got somebody to look for after this. It's somebody who might marry me."

At Claire's words, the three brothers looked at one another.

"Wha—? Did you ask some total stranger to marry you *again*?!"

"Close."

"Don't gimme 'close,' you moron! Just how many dolls do you think you've gotten to give you the brush-off that way, huh?!"

Berga sounded disgusted, but Claire answered him without seeming the least bit flustered.

"Now, hang on. I don't treat it like a pickup, and I'm not joking. I'm being serious, so there's no problem. And I'm positive I've gotten dumped up till now because there's an even better girl in my future. After all, this world is—"

"—'designed to work in my favor,' was it?"

Luck had probably heard those words several hundred times before. He'd responded with a simple question.

"That's right," Claire continued. "Anyway, I might get a good answer this time. Besides, if that one doesn't work out, I found another peach. If I get dumped this time, I think I'll try my luck with her next."

"You're as faithless as ever, too."

"Applesauce! I've never two-timed anyone, not even once. I've never gone out with a girl in the first place. I tell her I'm in love then and there, and if she says no, I move right on to the next one. If I get a yes, I'll be true to that girl the whole way. There's no problem with that."

In response to Claire—who'd delivered what was, in a way, a sound argument—Luck sighed, half in resignation.

"…I wish Firo would take a page from your book with regard to energy."

At the unexpected mention of his friend's name, Claire smiled nostalgically.

"Firo, huh? I'd like to see him. What about him?"

"He's been living with a girl he fancies for more than a year, but he hasn't told her he loves her or even kissed her yet."

"That's nuts… Is he actually human?"

Despite Claire's astonishment, his pace didn't slow at all.

"In any case, Claire. You really shouldn't trust the sort of woman who accepts an offer of marriage out of the blue."

Claire's response was to argue about the part of it that didn't matter:

"Claire's dead. Or he will be on paper, anyway, as far as the government's concerned."

He thought he'd come off sounding cool, but Luck jabbed him with a practiced comeback:

"If you're officially dead, you won't be able to marry that woman, you know."

At that, Claire stopped in his tracks, then turned around.

"Crap. What do I do? How much does it cost to buy an identity?"

"You aren't making any sense, Claire. In that case, what should we call you from now on?"

As Claire started walking again, he spoke casually:

"Well, maybe Vino... Or, you could call me the Rail Tracer."

"Lame."

In one of New York's back alleys, Berga and Claire began a violent brawl. Even as Keith watched them, his thoughts were with the struggle that was bound to grow fiercer from here on out.

This brawl was probably the last peaceful sight they'd see for a while. Still silent, Keith continued to gaze at the fight.

EPILOGUE
HOMICIDAL MANIACS

Edward the federal agent was receiving a report from a local police officer.

"I hear there were survivors."

"Yes, a man and a woman... We think they're probably members of the gang of robbers."

Information on the survivors was beginning to trickle in.

"And? How are they?"

"The woman's neck is hurt, but her life isn't in danger. The man is seriously injured; Bill is interviewing him at the hospital."

Next to the place where the survivors had been discovered, several police officers were standing around a certain object.

"So why is this pole broken?"

"I'd guess the survivors slammed into it."

"...Look, don't you think he punched it? I bet he did."

"I'm telling you, that's not even possible!"

"Yeah, but... You saw the man's arm, didn't you?"

"I saw it, so I can't completely rule it out. Is that guy a monster?"

"Either way, you know the only thing they'll be able to do for that arm is amputate it."

Remembering the horrible sight of the man's left arm, a few of the men felt sick again.

From the elbow down, all that remained of the surviving white suit's left arm was bone. The bones alone had stayed neatly behind, while the flesh had been blown clean off. His condition had been incredible to begin with, but there was something even more incredible than that:

The man was currently responding to an interview as though nothing had happened.

In a hospital a short distance away, Bill Sullivan was interviewing Ladd.

"Nn... Then you admit your crime?"

"Yeah, sure. Oh, just so's you know, all the guys I killed were in self-defense. I'll cop to everything about the attempted kidnapping, but make sure you get that bit down."

"Uh... Well, talk that over with the prosecutor and your lawyer."

As Bill was about to leave, Ladd tossed a question at his back:

"Do you know Huey Laforet?"

"Eh...... Mm. He is famous, after all."

"What pen are they putting him in?"

"Nn... That hasn't been settled yet, but I'd imagine it's going to be the Alcatraz military prison."

"Is that so? Thanks, pal."

"Ah... Take care of yourself. I'll introduce you to a prosthetic arm craftsman before the trial."

With that, Bill left the room.

Alcatraz, huh? That's a pretty decent opponent. I wonder how I can get 'em to put me in there, too. Keh-heh.

Imagining the pleasure he'd feel when he killed an immortal, Ladd fell asleep, an expression of ecstasy on his face.

EPILOGUE
TERRORIST GROUP

The new assistant to Fred, the doctor in gray, muttered quietly:

"Ahh, Ladd and Lua never did come back. I mean, it's those two, so they're probably alive, but…"

He'd been one of the white suits, but when the police had boarded the train, he'd asked Fred to make him his assistant and had escaped the long arm of the law that way. The delinquents beside them had glared at him, but they were criminals, too, so they didn't turn him over to the cops.

Afterward, he'd contacted the friend who'd been negotiating with the railway company on the outside, only to hear that the company had flatly vetoed their demands. Apparently, the black suits had been threatening the government, and some sort of pressure had been exerted on the railway company from that direction. He hadn't expected the strategy to succeed in the first place, but the idea that the black suits had been the cause of their failure made it particularly frustrating. Of course, not only was he still alive, he hadn't even been arrested. One would have had to admit that he'd been the luckiest member of the white suits.

He'd had nowhere to go, and in the end, it had been decided that he'd do odd jobs at Fred's hospital.

Having heard the former white suit's mutter, Fred answered, smiling quietly.

"Never mind. If they're alive, you'll see them again someday. As long as you all stay alive, someday, without fail… Come to think of it, that man was looking for someone, too."

"That man?"

"Yes, I ended up having to take a later train because I was treating him… Thanks to that, I wound up paying a lot for tickets. The treatment took quite some time, you see, and then the police put in an appearance as well."

"The cops?"

"Mm. When I was on my way to Chicago by car, I saw a tremendous explosion in the wasteland, off in the distance—"

⇔

Goose was alive.

Even enveloped in that hellfire, he'd miraculously escaped with his life.

I refuse to die in a place like this. I'll survive, and the secret of Huey's body will be mine—

Clinging to what little vindictiveness he had left, he crawled along the path by the tracks.

I should have comrades on this side. The ten who negotiated with the government, who weren't aboard the train. I saw the signal rocket go up when we reached the river. In other words, the government accepted our negotiations. Dammit, I was so close! Still, I'm not finished yet. With ten men, I'll be more than able to regain my balance—

Just then, over his head, a figure blocked his way.

"We've been looking for you, Goose."

I'm saved. Have my comrades found me?

When, thinking this, Goose raised his head, the spit that the figure had hocked up struck him in the face.

"Wha…?"

Goose was stunned. Standing there was a man with a huge burn on his face. It wasn't the only one. Large burn scars were visible on his neck and remaining hand as well, and on top of that, one of his hands had been cut off. It was an individual Goose knew all too well.

"...Nader...!"

It was the man who'd attempted to betray Goose before the operation, the man he thought he'd disposed of instead. A man who'd been caught up in the flames of the blast and who should have been burned to cinders by now.

"Yeah, I used the others' corpses to shield myself and managed to avoid dying instantly, but if a doctor hadn't been passing by just then, things could have gotten ugly... Although, even now, it's all I can do to stay on my feet."

Nader had handcuffs on his one wrist. A closer look revealed the figures of several police officers in the area. The officers didn't seem to have noticed Goose yet; they were searching the brush at random.

"It's a field inspection, Goose. I cut a little deal with the cops, see. In exchange for telling them about the plan and the negotiators' location, I get off with a suspended sentence. They can't make that public, of course. It sounds like they won't be making much about this incident public, period."

"Why...you..."

"Y'know, I hear those ten negotiators you were counting on just got arrested. My sincere condolences."

The burned man crouched down on the spot, putting his face close to Goose, whose expression was a mask of despair.

"You should've just killed me right there. You really weren't cut out for the military."

Those words were loaded with all of Nader's hatred and pity.

"You're completely pathetic, you failure."

Nader looked down on him, coldly. In response, Goose silently lowered his head. And then—

"Don't wander around on your own, Nader! We'll treat it as an escape attempt! ...Hmm? Is that a survivor?!"

Hastily, a police officer came running over. Nader sighed and answered him:

"Looks like he's dead. It just happened."

Goose's body had fallen facedown. A mixture of lots of blood and small fragments of flesh was flowing from his mouth.

Turning his back on the unmoving black suit, Nader walked away as if he'd lost interest.

"Ah, dammit, I've had it. I can't follow a guy who rushes to his own death like that. It looks like I'm really not cut out for this sort of thing. Maybe I'll go back to the country and help my dad with his cornfields..."

The young terrorist couldn't even visualize Goose's face anymore. In the end, apparently, that was all Goose had been.

Exposed to the freezing winter wind, the pitiful man's corpse was rapidly growing cold.

EPILOGUE
DELINQUENTS

The investigation had settled down, and the *Flying Pussyfoot* had been put in storage for a while.

Several figures stood quietly in the cars, from which the police had temporarily withdrawn.

"This ain't good."

"No, it really isn't."

Jon, the dining car bartender, and Fang, the cook's assistant, were the men who had told Jacuzzi's gang about the train. Technically, according to the original plan, they should have reached New York without anyone discovering this fact, but the situation had turned ugly on them.

"Think we'll get the boot?"

"We just might."

When Jacuzzi had recaptured the dining car from the black suits, the two of them had taken control with guns in their hands, as large as life. It had been glaringly obvious that they were used to using guns and, on top of that, that they were friends of the young guy who'd said he was occupying the train. Fortunately, because the cargo robbery that Jacuzzi's gang had pulled off hadn't been discovered, they'd managed to avoid a trip to the police station, but after everything was over, they'd been called out by the head cook. At the very least, that was what the two of them thought.

"If they fire us, what are you going to do?"

"My big sis is a waitress at a honey shop. Maybe I'll see if they'll hire me as a cook."

"What's this 'honey shop' business? And, anyway, didn't you cause trouble and get yourself run out of Chinatown?"

"They ran my sister out later. They said it was 'collective responsibility.' Then the Italians picked her up. From what I hear, there's a speakeasy in the back of the honey shop they run, and that's where she works."

As his pal spoke pragmatically, Jon murmured, gazing into empty space:

"Ah... A speakeasy, huh? I wonder if they're looking for bartenders, too."

With his listless voice as the last sound, a heavy silence pressed down around them.

A mouthwatering aroma drifted through the area around the counter seats where they were sitting. All they could hear from the depths of the kitchen was the sound of the head cook stirring a big pot of stew. It echoed in the silence, further amplifying Jon's and Fang's anxiety and appetite.

Abruptly, the noises from the kitchen ceased, and the head chef's bearlike voice resounded, quietly.

"You boys won't need to board this train tomorrow."

At those words, Jon and Fang sighed. In a way, their expressions seemed relieved.

"We're fired?"

They'd half expected that answer. Since they'd been prepared, the shock wasn't that great. However—

"Fired, hell. The whole dining car's being eighty-sixed."

"Huh?"

"Sir?"

At this, conversely, the two looked bewildered. The head cook paid no attention to them; his dispassionate voice just went on telling them the facts.

"The almighty company that gave us room as tenants is going to make it so this train never existed. In other words, their cheap trick to hush up the incident is costing you fellas your jobs. That goes for me, too, of course."

At this unexpected development, Jon and Fang looked at each other. In that case, why were they the only ones who'd been called here?

"I'm getting to that. I'm acquainted with some wealthy folks by the name of Genoard, and they're looking for a cook and bartender. I'm going to badger the owner of the main store into letting me go back there, so you two go work for the rich folks for a bit. They're flush enough to be hiring their own bartender. No complaints there, right?"

Jon's and Fang's eyes were round. Without even attempting to ask what they thought, the head cook forced the conversation ahead.

"I don't care what sort of gang you run with, or what kind of reprobates you are. You've got solid skills as a cook and bartender, and I'll vouch for those. Besides, you were the only duo with a bartender that I could think of. From what I hear, they're in their second home in New York right now, so head over and introduce yourselves tomorrow. Got it?!"

His tone brooked no argument, and Jon and Fang nodded in spite of themselves. However, deep down, they were also happy to hear they were trusted.

"Stew's ready. Eat up."

For the first time, the two responded in unison to the voice that came from the depths of the kitchen:

"Thank you, sir! We'll take it!"

However, at the head cook's next words, their smiles froze.

"Is that right. It's enough stew to feed a hundred people, and I was just worrying about how it was going to go to waste. That's a load off my mind. You said you'd eat it, so you better eat all of it. If you leave any leftovers, I'll stew your hands from the wrists down and make bouillon out of 'em, and don't you forget it."

⇔

"…And so we brought you a get-well snack. Eat. It'll give you energy."

190 BACCANO! VOLUME 3: 1931 THE GRAND PUNK RAILROAD: EXPRESS

"Not only that, it's delicious! If you don't eat this, you'll die! Because we'll curse you."

Behind a huge pot that contained easily over twenty-five gallons, Jon and Fang wore patently fake smiles.

"G-gimme a break."

On the other side of the pot, Jacuzzi was lying in bed, looking as if he was about to start crying in earnest.

Jacuzzi's bed was in a room of the hospital Fred ran. For now, they'd decided to admit him, but it sounded as if he'd be able to leave in a few days.

Jack was in the bed next to Jacuzzi, and Donny was asleep in the bed beyond that one. Both were snoring loudly. On Jon and Fang's orders, Donny had helped them carry the pot over, and while he was at it, he'd polished off enough of its contents to feed about twenty people.

Even so, the pot showed no sign of running out of stew. They'd been told it was enough for a hundred people, but they wondered if it might not actually be more than that.

Nice and Nick were there, too. In other words, all the friends who'd been on the train were here together. As they were discussing what to do about the stew, there was a sudden commotion outside the room.

"What's that? Something smells real good."

"Hey, no fair hogging it all for yourselves. Give us summa that, too."

At that, Jacuzzi's companions began to stream in through the door, one after another.

"Guys!"

Jacuzzi's voice was cheerful. Several of them were people who'd gone out in boats as the recovery team, to retrieve the explosives that had been dropped into the river.

"Yo, Jacuzzi! Those explosives! We got friends of ours, this old guy with a mine and a Hollywood movie tech, to buy them off us under the table. We sold 'em for sky-high prices! We're rollin' in dough! A hundred thousand dollars, man, a hundred thousand dollars! Don't that beat all?!"

"The clay shells from those grenades, too. With the contents taken out, those went for two hundred dollars apiece."

Jacuzzi loved his straightforward friends, who gave him a report on their finances before they worried about his injuries.

"Is that right? That's great!"

"But listen, Jacuzzi. You can't go back to Chicago no more."

Stuffing his face with the stew as if it was delicious, one of his friends told him the facts, pragmatically.

"Huh?"

"The mafia knows about all your rooms, and they'll fill you full of daylight just for going near one."

"O-oh no!"

Jacuzzi's face went white.

"Well, we're in New York already. Let's just stay. The other guys are on their way over."

"Nn, don't say that like it's easy…"

Jacuzzi's eyes had teared up, and his friends abruptly switched to a cheerful topic.

"Hey, by the way, Jacuzzi. Would you believe us if we told you a looker came falling down out of the sky?"

"Was it suicide?"

"*No*, you idiot! Look, we were picking up the cargo you guys dropped, right?! She was floating along, hanging on to one of those crates! She had a wounded shoulder, but she's a total stunner! She said, if we were gonna be in New York, she'd join up! She's a quiet, real polished doll, see? She just got the doc here to look at her injury."

"Huh. Really? I wonder if she got hurt during the train robbery."

After thinking for a little while, Jacuzzi artlessly warped the tattoo on his face.

"I'd like to meet her."

"Yeah, I'll introduce you. C'mon in, Chané!"

On seeing the beauty in the black dress who came in through the door, Jacuzzi welcomed his new friend with a bright smile—and Nice and Nick dropped their bowls of stew all over the floor.

EPILOGUE
THE FLYING PUSSYFOOT

A few days later   Somewhere in New York

"...And what did you gain by using half of that money to buy tickets?"

Somewhere in Chinatown. A voice spoke to Rachel, mixing with the sound of the ringing phones.

Rachel also answered in a shout that rivaled the voice.

"I don't know, sir. I was just very tired somehow."

Unusually for her, she was speaking politely. The listener was the president of the information brokerage with which she did business.

There were stacks of documents in the way, and she couldn't see his face. However, she was convinced he was smiling.

"Well, it's up to you whether you make use of that experience in the future or forget it."

"More than that, I regret that I didn't get to punch that whiskered pig myself."

Hearing the frustration in Rachel's voice, the information broker, whose face couldn't be seen, asked her a question:

"I have a little information regarding how the aftermath of that incident was dealt with. Would you like to hear it? —I won't charge you."

"I won't stand for it! I swear I'll take you to court! Over the security on that train, of course, and also over that business with the damned hick and the yellow monkey!"

The fat man with the little mustache was blustering. Once he'd come to after getting his shoulders dislocated by Claire, he'd spent the whole time in the bathroom, shaking with pain and terror. He'd been discovered by a squad of police officers after everything was over. When they'd popped his shoulders back into place, he'd bawled, and the passengers in the dining car had laughed at him.

He was an executive at a major railway company, and the humiliation had been hard for him to bear. As payback for that anger, he'd started to bring legal action against Nebra, the corporation that owned the train. However, someone had blocked that action at the last minute.

The person who had received the mustachioed man in the Nebra reception room was a middle-aged executive with a contradiction—an expressionless smile—plastered across his face.

"I'm afraid that won't do, Mr. Turner. We've paid sufficient reparations, and damaging the image of railway travel would prove unfortunate for you as well."

"That's irrelevant! This isn't about money for me—it's a matter of pride..."

Just then, the reception room telephone rang.

"I apologize for interrupting our discussion, but the call seems to be for you."

As he spoke, the executive remained expressionless. The mustachioed Turner grabbed the receiver away from him.

"It's me! Who the hell are...you...?"

On answering the telephone, Turner's expression changed dramatically. His face went pale, and as he continued the conversation, he broke out in a cold sweat. Before long, he put the receiver down, then glared at the executive with a fatigued expression.

"That's dirty. Bringing in politicians..."

"It seems that Senator Beriam also wants to keep the incident as quiet as possible. In this day and age, it's impossible to cover it up completely, but we can dilute its existence. There were no fatalities among the passengers during the incident, so we'd prefer not to draw too much attention to the matter."

"B-but…"

"Mr. Turner. I hear you once pinned the blame for your own mistake on a technician. We don't mind asking those technicians to testify again. If we tell them we'll hire them away on favorable terms, I'm sure they'll speak honestly."

Whiskered Turner went dead white, then left the room, unable to say another word.

The executive sent the final blow at his back:

"What goes around comes around, Mr. Turner. The senator has his eye on you. Unless you work very hard, your company will turn you into a sacrificial pawn…"

"…And that's how it is, or so I'm told. Does that make you feel a bit better?"

"How do you have information like that, sir?"

"I'm the one who sold the information on our whiskered pig's past to the executive. It was a trade."

In the midst of the ringing telephones, the voice spoke to Rachel quite casually:

"If you don't use information, it rots away. It's just like a craftsman's skills. Though I do feel bad about using information about your past without permission."

Rachel was silent for a while. Then she spoke, addressing the far side of the stacks of paper:

"May I bill you for travel expenses, starting next time? I'm not quite sure why, but I've decided to stop stealing rides."

"I don't mind in the least. That's fine. 'Not knowing why' is important. I think trusting your own senses is a very good thing."

Saying something quite unlike an information broker, at the very end, the voice from behind the documents added:

"Just don't forget your receipts."

⟺

Senator Beriam's political clout and the railway corporation's financial muscle were gradually making it as though the *Flying Pussyfoot* incident had never occurred. There had been one victim among the general public. A conductor had been discovered in the Chicago sewers, and his killer was still at large. The police weren't putting much effort into the investigation and had concluded that it was unrelated to the events on the *Flying Pussyfoot*.

The culprit had already left this world behind.

The faceless corpse that had been found in the conductors' room was assumed to be Claire Stanfield.

The train itself was scrapped, except for the locomotive, and its cars stood quietly in a public park on the outskirts of the city.

Strangely, there was one bit missing from those cars. After they were put on display, someone had taken a piece from the roof of the last one.

Then came December 5, 1933.

On that day, when the Prohibition Act was repealed, people danced for joy on the train and smashed it up, after which it mingled with the scrap iron in the junkyard and vanished.

The *Flying Pussyfoot*—or "flying prohibition enforcer"—had swaggered across the whole of America along with the Prohibition Act.

In contrast with the demise of the act, its end was far too lonely.

The stage of the incident was covered up, going from darkness into darkness, and no one ever knew what had become of it.

...Except for one piece: the message that had been cut out of the roof.

Baccano! 1931—The End

AFTERWORD

First, thank you very much for reading this section, too, even though it has nothing to do with the main story.

I'm sorry about always starting these the same way, but as usual, I have absolutely no idea what to write in an afterword.

However, lately, I'm told that the number of people who decide whether to buy the book by looking at the afterword is on the rise. I wonder... What if the author's the sort of writer whose afterwords and main stories are completely different in everything from style to atmosphere? Are there people who, after they make their purchase, think, *I was tricked by the afterword!* and cry all over the book? I'm really concerned about that.

—But I digress.

All right: In this story, for almost all of it, I moved things along within the confines of a train.

The train gimmick has been depicted in media in all sorts of genres, and I think the really interesting part is the uniqueness of the train element itself. I've always been fascinated by how this set—which you could call a moving locked room—is used in a variety of stories in a variety of fields, and each time, it's used in a different way. There really are an infinite number of ways to use it, mixing in similes and metaphors about the changing scenery and the travelers, the rails and roads. I think when railways are used as stage devices, it's particularly easy for these things to show up clearly.

I've been thinking constantly about how someday I'd like to write a story that uses a train in a different way from the one I've used here.

---

* This is the second volume of a two-part story. For those of you who read it and thought, "I only read this one, and I didn't really get it," please take a look at *Baccano!: 1931 The Grand Punk Railroad: Local*, released in August.

*   *   *

In this story, I wrote about incidents that occurred during the same time frame as the previous book but focused on different characters and showed things from different perspectives.

This isn't especially original: Changing the perspective is a technique that's used in all sorts of genres. Lately, I get the impression that it's used particularly often in games. As I wrote, I thought, *I want to use this structure, which is one of a huge variety of techniques, to write a story that's as dumb as possible.* I can't even begin to imagine how readers took it, though.

"It's a pointless, dumb story... But it's fun." If they said that, I think it would be the best compliment ever. At least for books with the *Baccano!* title, I plan to focus on creating that sort of story.

Parenthetically, when I first showed my editor, Suzuki, the manuscripts for *Local* and *Express*, he said, briefly, "It's loco." ...What does he want from me?

I'd like to write all sorts of other things in the future, from more long series to one-shot stories, and I want to get good enough to write dumb stories and stories that aren't dumb, stories with absolutely no substance and stories with quite a lot of substance, and stories with all sorts of different orientations.

At the very least, as I work every day to make sure the good people of the sales department don't threaten me with demon masks and the words *Your books don't sell, so quit writing*, I want to keep writing stories that ultimately have some sort of influence, both on myself and on the people who are kind enough to read them. That's my current goal.

Rrgh...... I'm pretty sure I remember writing something like this last time...

In any case, I'll follow the example of the other Dengeki Bunko authors and experiment with different things in an attempt to establish my own unique afterword style, so please humor me.

* As usual, everything past this point is thank-yous.

*   *   *

Regarding this release: To Chief Editor Suzuki, for whom I'm constantly causing trouble, and to the good people of the sales, PR, and editing departments.

To the proofreaders, who always check for typos, dropped characters, and ungrammatical sentences.

To my family, friends, and acquaintances, particularly everyone in S City, who help me out in all sorts of ways.

To Okayu and Torishimo, who helped me at HP, and to "bludgeoning" supervising editor Unimaru.

To Katsumi Enami, who draws characters that seem to evolve every time I see new pictures, and whose fantastic illustrations took this book to the next level.

And to the people I mustn't forget: the readers who picked up this book.

Thank you so much, this time and always!

From here on out, I think I'll work on moving both my stories and my afterwords in all sorts of different directions. I hope you'll stick with me on this leisurely journey as we travel from station to station…

June 2003, at my place
Playing the opening animation of *PARTY 7* (directed by Katsuhito Ishii) on repeat.

Ryohgo Narita

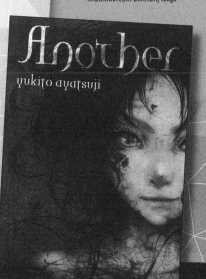